Overl

The Boneyard Brotherhood MC

By Amber Burns

Published by
Scarlet Lantern Publishing

SCARLET LANTERN
Publishing

Copyright © 2016 by Amber Burns & Scarlet Lantern
Publishing
All rights reserved.

This is a work of fiction. Names, characters, businesses,
places, events and incidents are either the products of the
author's imagination or used in a fictitious manner. Any
resemblance to actual persons, living or dead, or actual
events is purely coincidental.

This book contains sexually explicit scenes and adult
language.
All characters in this work are 18 years of age or older.

Prologue

I didn't find the Boneyard Brotherhood. The Boneyard Brotherhood found me. I had been at the end of my leash, using alcohol as a means to self-medicate due to all the things that had followed me home from my last tour in Iraq. I hadn't considered much after my therapy, aside from surviving to the next day. But there was more to life than just surviving. I kept many of the ole' Army routines including shaving and maintaining a cut that would keep any soldier out of trouble. Routines had been drummed into me since boot camp, and I wasn't ready to let go of them because of a medical discharge. I had planned on being a lifer and I was going for the full twenty years... maybe beyond. But war and life had different plans for me.

Fortunately, life sent me a savior just when I was bent over a bar top considering the flavor of the nine millimeter I kept at home.

"I've seen that look before," a gruff voice cut through the drunk fog that had surrounded my brain. There's a reason why they tell you not to consume alcohol while on some medications. "You're at rock bottom and ready to call it quits."

I pushed up from the bar to glare at the person intruding on my wallowing in self-pity, ruining my contemplation of suicide.

"Fuck off," I slurred; I really didn't want to be bothered.

"Aye, soldier boy, don't snap at me just yet." The voice was attached to a grisly man, the majority of his hair was on his face. He was sporting a receding hairline as if hair on his head had decided it'd rather be on his face. "I see a man that's down for the count, and I'm tryin' ta give you a hand up. Do you want it?"

I squinted at him as I tried to decipher what he was saying as it didn't immediately make sense to me. "What do you mean?"

"You okay with riding bitch? I want to show you something." He looked away from me to the bartender that had been serving me watered down beers. They were so weak it had taken more than a few to get me feeling this way. "He paid up?"

"Yep, he paid after each drink," the bartender said. He was an older man that made me think of my dad each time he gave me a new beer. I got a look that said I should reconsider my life, but it didn't keep him from giving me the beer even when I went under the table.

"Okay, kid." He hoisted me off of the barstool with a hand under one arm, and was kind enough to catch me when I stumbled and nearly fell. "I'm going to show you a better way to deal with shit, and you're going to thank me when I do." He took me out to the curb and gestured to a sleek motorcycle that sat next to it. At the time, I had no idea about make or model. "Look at that beauty."

"You interrupted my beer for a bike?" I asked because it sounded crazy. "How is this," I gestured to the bike and tried not to wear my issues on my sleeve when I asked the question, "supposed to help me?"

He handed me a helmet and put a bandana over his bald head before putting on a helmet himself. "It's not just the bike, boy," he said gruffly, giving me a look that said I was close to insulting him. "It's the ride that sets you free. If you weren't so shit faced, I'd let you drive it, but I would have to kill you if you dropped it. And I like ya, I don't want to have to kill ya." He straddled the bike and gave the seat behind him a pat, grinning at me. "So, you get to ride bitch."

Who does he think he is? He doesn't know me. I just looked at the helmet in my hands, felt the ache in my back, and wondered just how this would help. But so far, my options were nil. I was just considering chewing on a gun. What's one ride before I go? I put the helmet on, and after a little awkward maneuvering on my part, I managed to get on the seat behind him.

"What's your name?" I asked before the engine would drown me out.

"Ted," he said with a feral grin as he kicked the bike to life. "You call me Teddy, son, and I'll gut check ya."

He didn't give me any more warning. He started to ease the bike onto the road, and the roar of the engine seemed to drown out every thought I had. I held onto the seat, not comfortable putting my hands on another man, and let the wind whip into my face. After the first bug smacked me, I learned to close my mouth. I was still drunk and I wasn't ready to hurl on a moving vehicle. Fortunately, six years of MREs gave me a gut of steel and nausea didn't rear its ugly head. I surrendered to the sound of the roaring bike and the whistling wind. The lingering effects of the alcohol drifted away from me and I became drunk on the free feeling that was created by riding down the road. I had no clue how fast he was going and I didn't care either. I didn't realize just how much I was enjoying the ride until he eased us to a stop outside a little cinderblock building that was surrounded by motorcycles.

"Why stop?" I asked, feeling like I got gypped. I wasn't ready to face the reality that was already coming back to me.

"We got where we were going, kid." He shot me a grin over his shoulder like he knew this would be my reaction. "So," he shifted a little so he could get a better look at me, "this the hand up you needed?"

"I've got to get me one of these," I assured him, purposely ignoring his question.

He laughed out loud, causing the bike we sat on to rock a little. He was a little bit on the heavy side.

"That's the reaction I thought I'd get. C'mon. Get off the bike and I'll introduce you to the rest of The Brotherhood. Then we'll see what we can do about getting you a bike and getting your feet on the ground for good." He helped me off the bike and walked it to a spot that he intended to park it. "So, fresh meat, what's your name?"

I didn't even question it when he called me "fresh meat." I accepted it wholeheartedly. He mentioned 'The Brotherhood' and it must of meant that I was about to become a part of it.

"Private Second Class Sidney Redding," I said like the drunk shit that I was. I might have even saluted him. I was honestly surprised he didn't slap me.

He let out a heavy laugh, clearly amused by my introduction.

"Shit, you are fresh. Drop the Army ranks, kid. I ain't been in since Desert Storm. If you ever blurt that shit out again, I'll be sure to knock a knot in your head." He took a breath, shot me a grin, and jerked the door open. "Welcome home, Sid."

1

It had been four years since I met Teddy and I haven't looked back or thought about chewing on my gun since. Teddy had been right. And yeah, he told me not to call him that. But the man was like a teddy bear despite the huff-and-puff front he put on. Riding a motorcycle had been the best way to free myself from all of my problems. I was to the point that I was comfortable with letting go of the anti-depressants and the anti-anxiety medicines that didn't even seem to work for me. They only made me a drooling zombie anyway. I was embraced by a band of brothers; each from one of the military branches and each retired or discharged for various reasons. I think the reason why Teddy picked me up off that barstool was because he saw the mess that I was, saw me struggling, and gave me a purpose I hadn't had since I was discharged. I was taught how to be a civilian again by men that had been exactly where I was.

It was a sweet relief. A relief I needed.

I spent the majority of my days working on bikes. Someone had learned I was a mechanic while in the Army and that I was pretty good with engines, so I got put to work. I was back to living with grease and oil on my hands and it was something I was good with. Nothing I was going to complain about. My dues got paid by the other members in exchange for the work I did. I was certain that the club held the look of an innocent gathering for retired military guys, but they also dabbled in other things to raise money. Money that was raised paid for the building and the chicks that worked the bar and grill. I got a stipend, too; under the table since I did the majority of the *work* around the bar.

I didn't really get involved in all the illegal shit. Teddy said he didn't want to endanger my disability, which was essentially what I lived off of now. The injury I suffered that got me discharged was some serious nerve damage in my back and left leg, fucked it up good. So while I would go out on group rides through the territory and act as general muscle when necessary, I stayed out of anything illegal going on in the club. Well, outside of hitting a smoldering joint when it was passed to me, of course.

I was satisfied with the work that I did and I steadily let go of the routine I had been clinging to. I finally let my hair grow out. And although I couldn't let it get shaggy like some of these bastards did, it wasn't the buzz cut I used to sport. Along with that, I managed a respectable beard, something I enjoyed to no end. It felt good to not have to shave anymore.

As I got broken in I started collecting tattoos, which was an acquired taste. One might say it became an addiction; an addiction to cover as much of my skin as I could. I looked less and less like a broken soldier and more like the hairy bear of a man that picked me up in a bar. In a non-sexual way, just to clarify.

I was doing what I could to make the club shine and keep everyone's wheels turning. I loved every minute of it. I made sure my gratitude showed through with the work that I did. Even though the bar only serviced the Brotherhood, I made sure it stayed running better than any Navy ship.

"You ever consider getting into custom bikes?" Jimmy, a new member that was working on getting patched in asked.

He served four years in the Air Force and didn't mention what exactly he did or why he got out. For the most part he hovered around me, running for parts when I needed them and shining other member's bikes. It took a little bit of work off my hands, so I didn't complain.

"The fuck do I know about making custom bikes?" I had oil damn near up to my elbows as I was reassembling the engine of Wilson's Honda. "I just do engines, man." I paused to shoot him a look. "Remind me to knock a knot in this asshole's head for letting his shit get this messed up."

It got a laugh out of the kid and he shook his head. "You think you can take him? I heard he is into boxing and was a Marine. I know it's probably been twenty years, cuz he's old as fuck, but I bet he can still beat ass. Fucker is meaner than a pit bull."

"Probably." I shrugged it off.

"What were you? A ranger? Green beret or some shit?" He did this occasionally, poking at me as he tried to figure out if I was worth idolizing.

"Nope." I went back to focusing on the task at hand. I didn't care if I disappointed him. "Just a mechanic."

"Oh." He sounded unimpressed, but I ignored it.

I didn't need to impress some kid. He'd ask questions about my injuries, but there were some things you don't ask questions about that. War stories and injuries are a few of those things and Jimmy didn't always understand that.

A car pulled into the little lot that was in front of the bar. Its driver seemed to struggle to find a parking spot before giving up and shutting off the engine. I curled a lip... it sounded like it needed some work done. When a woman stepped out of it I wasn't surprised in the least. Not to be sexist, but women often didn't take care of their cars. Jimmy and I watched the little thing approach the door to the bar curiously as she held one of those thick orange envelopes. She was short, at most maybe five three, and probably struggled to weigh one hundred and twenty soaking wet. But still, she managed to have some curves on her. That ass had my undivided attention, even with her trying to hide it.

"Who the fuck is that?" Jimmy asked; she had his attention, too. "She doesn't look like an old lady."

No, no she didn't. She wore a flared black skirt that hung down to her knees and a modest blouse, like she was trying too hard to cover up all her assets.

"I don't know." I pushed myself up and started to saunter over to meet her. There was a slight limp to my step and it was something that I would have to live with due to my wartime injuries. I took a red rag from my back pocket and made the useless effort of cleaning my hands. "Hey, Sweetcheeks," I called out to her. I wanted her attention for a number of reasons. "You need something?"

She stopped and looked at me, green eyes opening wide behind her thick-rimmed glasses. She looked struck like a deer caught in headlights. Her face was heart shaped with rosy cheeks and lips that I would kill to have wrapped around my dick. That's the first place my mind went, and I couldn't fathom why. With as fucked up as my back was, I didn't frequent erections just at the sight of a pretty girl. But here the ole' boy was standing at attention like fucking magic. Her mouth opened and closed as if she were mimicking a fish out of water. I waited, and I felt Jimmy come up behind me to appreciate the girl as I had. Something bristled in me at that and I shot him a glare. I didn't say it, but he knew I was calling dibs.

"I uh," she finally managed words. "I am... I'm looking for Theodore Tillman," She finally said, looking afraid of the two of us. I know we're obviously bikers, but we're not that scary.

"Theodore Tillman?" Jimmy echoed in confusion.

"Ted," I clarified before nodding at her. "He ain't here right now. What you got for him? I'll be sure to get it to him."

"I," she started to stutter again and fidgeting with the envelope in her hands, "I-I need his signature."

"You servin' him papers?" Jimmy asked with a laugh like the idea was funny.

He was a kid, he didn't know better. If the lady hadn't been here, I would've had to give him a hard kick in the ass. Instead, I gave him a hard look, then made a pointed glance towards Teddy's chopper in the corner. Hopefully, the kid caught on. I looked back at the girl floundering in front of us.

"He'll be here tomorrow between ten and six," I informed her. "After six I can't make promises. If I can't drop the papers off for you, you'll have to come back here with that pretty face of yours."

Jimmy didn't correct me but sniggered obnoxiously when the girl turned several shades of red. Fucker was ruining my flirting game.

"T-thanks." She turned to run back in the direction of her car, affording us a better look at her legs and backside. She was short, but she had a pair of legs on her.

"Hey, Sweetcheeks," I hollered after her. "You gonna give us your name, so we know who to tell him came-a-callin'?" I couldn't help but grin when she looked back at me all wide-eyed. I got that deer caught in headlights look again. "Or should I just keep callin' you Sweetcheeks?"

"Madison Ells," she said as she eyed me frightfully, like I was going to bite her or something.

I licked my lips and I saw her face turn a brighter shade of red, so maybe that was what she thought. Maybe I would take a bite out of her; I wouldn't mind getting a little taste.

"I'll hope to see ya tomorrow then, Madi." I grinned at her. She squeaked a farewell and sat back into her car. She backed out of the parking lot and sped off, the squeal her car made gave me a reason to grimace. "What is it with women and their inability to take care of their cars?"

"Are you diagnosing her car?" Jimmy sounded amused watching her, too. "She was cute but far too meek for me. I prefer a hellcat."

"Never," I looked at him with a grin, "ever judge a book by its cover. You never know how a woman is in bed until you take her for a ride." I gave his shoulder a pat not caring about the mess that was on my hands. "Go get me a spark plug or two for Wilson's bike. I'm gonna go let Teddy know his old lady is finally making the move to cut the chain."

"You think that's what it is?" He made a noise, sounding disgusted as he started to make his way to his bike. "You sure it ain't something more sinister?"

"Pft, like Teddy has a sinister bone in his body." I opened up the barroom door. "Honda Shadow, '85. Make sure you get the right part or you're gonna have to turn your ass around and get a new one."

I didn't give him the chance to question it further. Plus, I didn't want to spend the rest of the day working on Wilson's bike.

"Yea, yea, yea," Jimmy grunted as he started his bike up and wheeled it out of the lot, revving it up so that it made an obnoxious amount of noise.

I didn't wait for him to speed off; I went into the bar and let out a sigh of relief. Sometimes the kid irked my nerves and this was a much-needed break. I sauntered over to the bar and gave it a knock, seeing Cindy in the kitchen fussing with what I assumed was the dinner menu.

"Hey, Lady!" I hollered back at her to get her attention. "You got Teddy locked up in the fridge back there?"

"Shit!" She let out a string of expletives that would make a sailor blush, and there were sailors present. I couldn't help, but grin. "Goddamnit, boy!"

She stood in the kitchen doorway to glare at me. Cindy was older, probably in her fifties, and I was sure she came with the building. Her hair was bleached blonde, despite her age, and she sported a little roundness in the middle and on her hips. It didn't keep the rest of the boys from hitting on her.

"I damn near cut myself," she called out. "What do you want?"

"Teddy," I repeated slowly. She had a temper on her and I took great pleasure in egging her on. There was something fun about getting her to threaten me. "You finally do him in and hide him in the fridge?"

"No, but I have half a mind to do that to your ass," she huffed then nodded towards the other side of the bar room. "He's in the office with Wilson. I think they're having a serious talk so if you need someone to mouth off to you'll have to find someone else."

"Hey, hey, hey." I started to back away, raising my hands as if to placate the woman. "I don't mouth off to anyone but you, Lady. You're my favorite."

"I ain't buyin' your shit, pretty boy," she growled in return.

"I'll wait for you," I snickered as I ducked back to the office door.

I watched as Cindy went back to the kitchen and I knocked. I was playing with fire and I knew it. One of these days I was betting she'd hold me up with one of her kitchen knives. But, women like her were all fiery and so hard to resist messing with.

"Come in," Wilson bellowed, and I opened the door. "Redding, the hell are you doing here? My bike better be running."

Wilson was a Marine sergeant at one point. He served in a war, probably 'Nam, but I couldn't pinpoint it for sure because he looked like leather. I couldn't guess his age to save my life.

"I gotta heads up for Teddy." I looked at the older man that had ushered me into the club.

Teddy wasn't near as old as Wilson, but he had admitted to serving in Desert Storm, so I figured he was in his mid-fifties. They both looked weathered and it was hard to guess, the military did that to you though.

"Boy," he growled at me, "what did I tell you about calling me that?"

"Still waiting on that gut check, man," I admitted. I cleared my throat and sobered though because I wasn't sure how he was going to take the news I was about to give. There was no easy way to break it. "A girl drove up a minute ago with papers that she needed you to sign for. I think she was trying to serve you."

His features went blank, he put on a poker face and he gave a nod as he looked away. "That … that might be it. Damn," he breathed out and grimaced. "I didn't expect her to go through with it. I thought it was just an empty threat like all the others."

I waited in the doorway, my heart going out to the guy. Aside from the sweet looking girl I just saw, I hadn't had a steady woman since before I went to Iraq. I hadn't even been interested in one. I couldn't imagine how it felt when the woman you pledged your life to suddenly wanted to call it quits.

"I'm sorry, man." It was all I could offer. "D'ya want me to get you a beer?"

Wilson reached across the desk to give Teddy a solid slap on the back. "We're here for ya, brother. You're not facing this shit alone."

He nodded, though it was evident that he was going to get emotional. "Nah, Sid, I don't need a beer. Thanks."

"Let me get Wilson's bike back together and we'll go for a ride." I paused then remembering the details. "Girl is going to be back tomorrow with the papers. I told her you'd be here between ten and six. That cool?"

"Why didn't you just let her bring them to me?" he asked, not sounding angry but looking curious.

"I like you knowing what's coming before it gets here." I shrugged. "Plus... she was kinda hot."

"Oh," he gave me a shark-like smirk, "I could use a hot piece of ass if I'm going to be free of the old ball and chain."

"Sorry, fucker," I started to step back, "already called dibs."

That got a laugh from both of them, and I went back outside. Nothing like a night ride to get the feels off your shoulders. I had some work that I needed to finish.

2

At ten on the dot, little Miss Ells showed back up at the bar. I was surprised, but happy because I was out in the yard cleaning up my own bike. For some reason I wanted her to see me next to my pride and joy: a '94 Dyna Wide Glide. I had slaved and saved every penny I could pinch for this beauty. She was a brilliant silver, and if I could make love to a motorcycle, I would definitely be trying to shove my cock into my silver girl.

Sex with inanimate objects aside, the current object of my attention pulled into the lot just like she did the other day, parking right in the middle of it. We didn't really cater to cars. Hers still sounded like it was riding like shit. She got out and gave me a cautious look. I did nothing but offer her my best grin. At least I still had all my teeth, not all the fuckers in the club could say that.

"Morning, Sweetcheeks," I winked at her.

She blushed and then she gave me a nod.

"Morning. I told you my name yesterday," she tried to go for stern, but it faltered as her voice quaked, "so you wouldn't call me that."

"Oh." I gave the gas tank one last swipe with the cloth before stuffing it into the back pocket of my jeans. "You sure did," I said as I approached her. "Do you think I forgot it?"

She laughed shakily then shrugged. "Honestly, it wouldn't surprise me."

Today she chose to wear another long sleeved, button up blouse and a pencil skirt. She looked as if she was trying to blend in and not garner any attention. However, she sure caught my eye.

"Miss Madison Ells." I put on my most charming grin. "I wouldn't say that's forgettable. C'mon lets get you to Teddy." I gestured towards the bar door. She started forward and I instantly put my hand to the small of her back, guiding her along. She tensed and paused so that my hand was against her with a bit more pressure. I looked down at her and raised an eyebrow. "Okay?"

That pretty blush of hers had me thinking all kinds of wrong things. Another day that my pecker decided that he'd been down and out for long enough. She had his full undivided attention in a way the vibrating engine of my bike never did. She didn't protest, but she looked up at me with those big green eyes. Shit, I was in trouble. What was I going to do after she served her papers and got her signature?

We started moving again and I struggled to think of a way to get her to come back. Maybe I could find out where she worked and pay her a visit. Was that too much? Would that put me right into creeperville? I stepped ahead of her and opened the door for her so she could go in first.

"I'll take ya right to him," I promised.

"This is a bar?" she asked looking away from me and around the room.

"Kinda." I didn't bother to elaborate. I nodded towards one the doors in the back part of the bar, close to obvious bathrooms. "Teddy's in the office. But, a piece of advice, dude gets pissy if you call him Teddy."

"Why do you call him Teddy?" she asked, eyeing me curiously. I hoped that I had her attention like she had mine.

"I think it's fun to piss him off and I can take a punch." I tapped on the door. "If you called him Teddy and he started swinging, I'd have to lay him flat and I dunno how he'd handle that."

"What?" Wilson barked.

I didn't bother reporting anything I just opened the door. "Teddy's got a visitor."

"I'm really starting to regret dragging your drunk ass out of that bar," Ted groaned from the other side of the table. He sat up when he saw the girl I brought with me, and I could see the appreciation in his gaze. Though I had to admit, Madison looked like she could probably be his daughter. "This the girl you told me about yesterday?"

"Yep." I ushered her further into the room so she could handle her business. "You remember what I said yesterday?"

He snorted and eyed Madi, as I'd taken to call her, with a more serious expression.

"What have you got for me?"

"I'm a representative of Mister Fredrick Stevens who is representing Doris Tillman." Her voice quaked a little and I suspected it had something to do with being in a room with three bikers. She offered him the thick, orange envelope. "I can imagine the frustration, and I'm very sorry for inconveniencing you, but I need your signature to prove that you received this."

He gave her a hard look, and I thought for a second he was going to give her trouble. I glowered, edging closer to her. Teddy noted the movement and raised an eyebrow. "You gotta pen, Private?"

I snorted and fished one out of my back pocket before I offered it to him. I watched Madi curiously as she waited patiently for the slip of paper that said she had done her job. Teddy handed it over before giving me a look. "Alright, you got your shit. You can go."

"Th-thank you," she stuttered.

"You're such a gentleman, Teddy," I grumbled as I opened the office door.

"Tell that to my soon to be ex-wife." He gave me the one-fingered salute before he turned back to the papers on the desk before him.

I'd have to check on him later, but first, there was something more important. I ushered Madi out of the office and closed the door behind us.

"Sorry about that," I apologized on Teddy's behalf. "He's usually like a teddy bear and not so damn ornery."

She cleared her throat and had my full attention. "The reaction was appropriate. I assume you don't understand because you've not been in his position. There's nothing pleasant about getting served divorce papers."

She carefully folded the paper that held Teddy's signature. She fidgeted and made no effort to meet my gaze. Her shyness appealed to me in a way I didn't understand, but I wanted to explore just how shy and innocent she was. Only, I wasn't that much of an asshole that I would push her out of her comfort zone in a public place.

"Divorce," she began again as I walked her through the bar, "is not a pleasant thing."

"I guess I'll find out with the way Teddy handles it." I made sure to hold the door open that led outside for her. I would be a perfect gentleman even if I didn't look it. "Hopefully it's not something I'll ever find out about first hand." I followed her to her car and I couldn't tell whether or not I was making her uncomfortable.

"Thank you," she said uneasily, speaking without stumbling over her words. "I appreciate your help."

I guess being outside must have been helping. Maybe it was the fact that there were fewer people out here. She went to her car door and opened it, getting ready to drive off, and I knew I'd probably never see her again.

Fuck that, I told myself. *Not gonna have that.*

I stood at the front of her car and gave the hood a slight knock. "This thing is running funny. You need to get it looked at."

I got a deer caught in headlights look from her again. She shook her head before dropping her gaze from mine.

"I don't have the money for a mechanic right now." She frowned and I felt like an ass for pointing it out. "I know it sounds bad, I keep putting it off in hopes it'll last me a little bit longer."

"Well," I tried to give her my best grin, "it's your lucky day, Sweetcheeks. I just happen to work on engines. You take me to lunch and I'll take a look at your car, free of charge."

"I thought if I told you my name you weren't going to call me that." She looked at me again, her brows drawing down together and the look she gave me made me want to tug her out of her shell. There was potential here with her, and I definitely couldn't let her get away.

"Force of habit," I shrugged. "It means you have a nice ass. If it bothers you, we're good with me calling you Madi, right?"

She did have a nice ass, at least from what I could tell with the clothes that she wore. They weren't tight and didn't show off her figure, so I had to use my imagination. Her face flushed as I leaned forward onto the hood of her car.

"M-Madi's fine."

"Am I gonna get lunch out of you to look at your car?"

She looked hesitant, and I was afraid that I lost my chance with her. She pulled out her phone from her bag and looked at it. "I take lunch at one."

I took the opportunity to pull my own phone from a pocket and offered it to her. "Gimme your number and we can arrange for me to give your car the once over and see what it takes to get it fixed."

She looked uncertain, but took my phone and swiped it to the contacts. I watched as she programmed her name and number into it before she offered it back to me.

"Do you have an idea what it is?" she asked.

"It could be your transmission," I said honestly as I took my phone. I wanted to send her a text to be certain the number was actually hers. I kept it simple, a 'hi beautiful' seemed to be just enough. "Have you had any problems shifting gears or anything like that?"

She jumped a little when her phone vibrated. It let me know she got my message, especially when she turned pink.

"Not that I've noticed. The only thing I've noticed is the funny noise."

That didn't say a lot. Sometimes when it came to cars women tended to ignore a lot.

"Okay, we'll see when I get the chance to look at it. Text me," I said seriously as I put my phone away. "I am holding you to this lunch thing. I'd like to look at this," I tapped at the hood of her car, "today if you don't mind."

"I get off of work at five." She shifted from foot to foot. "I need to get back. Thank you, I-I guess I'll see you at lunch."

"Yep."

I watched her sit and I stepped away from her car. She pulled out and I checked my phone for the time. I had a couple of hours to wait to see her again and I was gonna be antsy. I went back to the building with my phone in my hand, pulling up a website on the make of her car. I was hoping that it wasn't the transmission. Maybe it just needed to be flushed.

"Did you get a date out of that girl?" Jimmy asked standing just outside of the bar door. "Man, I didn't know you had skills."

"I got skills," I said without looking from my phone. "This limp ain't just from an IED, son. My dick is so big it affects the way I walk." I nudged him with my shoulder. "Women recognize it and want to get a piece."

"You're so full of shit." He shook his head with a laugh.

"Blue eyes, dude." I pulled on my cheek to emphasize my eye color. "I ain't full of shit. Unlike your brown-eyed ass. My dick is so big I could win a three-legged race by myself."

He laughed louder at that. "With the way you hobble around here, I doubt it." He pulled a cigarette out from the stash he had rolled up in his sleeve. He offered me one but I waved it off. I was on a fixed income and couldn't really afford a vice like smoking. "How'd you manage to talk her into seeing you?"

I shrugged and leaned back against the building, standing beside him. "You gotta question these good looks?" I gestured to himself and gave the beard I had a slight tug. "Honestly, grow yourself one of these and women will throw themselves at you."

He scratched his chin and jaw like he was contemplating my advice. "I got peach fuzz right now."

"It's a work in progress." I patted his shoulder. "Grow a beard and the women will come."

"Got any work to do today?" He stuck the cigarette in his mouth and let it dangle from his lip as he spoke. "Or is it a day off and you're just so fucking sad that you got nowhere to go?"

"Motherfucker I gotta lunch date." I straightened and wavered on my feet slightly, a spasm started at the small of my back, and I gritted my teeth to keep from cursing more. "I ain't sad. I'm fucking ecstatic."

"I got a friend that just picked up a piece-of-shit bike that needs work," he cut in, apparently not seeing me falter or he didn't care. "He's willing to pay."

I took a breath through my teeth as I tried to shake off the pain. "So he's not part of the club?"

Jimmy shook his head. "He's never served. Unless Ted and Wilson are considering taking in civis? Then I'd definitely vouch for the guy."

"You haven't even been patched in yet, dude." I shrugged then stretched, trying to get some relief as I reached my hands up to hit the roof's overhang. "I got no problems looking at the guy's bike. All my tools are here so he'll have to bring it here. You'll have to okay that with Teddy." I turned to go inside, deciding I'd need to take something and maybe sit down with my trusty TENS unit for some much-needed relief. "I got plans for today, but I could probably see the guy before five."

Jimmy pulled something out of his pocket and offered it to me. It took me a second to realize it was money. "I'll send him a text to be here at three, so you can give it a good look. Then you can make a list of parts you might need so he can get them for you."

I took the money and my eyebrows rose. The kid had given me two hundreds just for saying I'd look at his friend's bike.

"Where'd you get this?" I questioned.

"Side jobs, man." He smirked at me. "If Teddy wasn't protecting your disability claim you could do them, too." He opened the door for me, cigarette still on his lip. "You do me this favor, and I'll pay you three hundred more if you get his bike fixed."

"Is it a project bike?"

"Nah, I think he dropped it or some shit. It doesn't look like it really needs body work, but the engine is definitely fucked." He shrugged. "You'll probably be able to tell when you look at it."

I nodded as I went inside, stuffing the money he gave me into a pocket and deciding it was better to get relief than to question him. The spasms shifted lower, and I had about two hours to get some sense of normality before I tried to get Madi's attention.

Girls dig oily guys, right?

3

After a few pills and nearly an hour with a TENS unit taped to my lower back, the pulsing aches faded to a more tolerable level. I went to the men's room to get myself cleaned up and try my best to make an impression. I combed out the beard and did my best to make my growing mop of hair settle down. I couldn't keep it too long, but it was getting shaggy. Luckily I didn't look beastly like some of the guys that rolled through here. Though covered in tattoos, I was definitely the exact opposite of Madi. She looked the picture of innocence, and the way she stuttered and fidgeted, I had to wonder if she had ever had a man's attention before. I'd figure it out.

I got a text from her that gave me about thirty minutes to get to her. It was an address and that was about it. No 'hi how are you?' or any kind of small talk. Damn, she knew how to shoot a guy's ego down a notch. I didn't let it get to me though. I saddled up on my bike, put my helmet on, and kicked my baby into a roar. The ride to the address she gave me was only a short fifteen minutes, but the rumble and vibrations of the motorcycle between my legs were enough to help the achiness.

By the time I got there, I was high from the breeze that I had ridden through, and I was just basking in the fact that it had been such a great day to go for a ride. I wonder what the chances were that I could talk Madi on to the back of my bike. It was a tempting thought that I would definitely be taking a shot at. I pulled up to a curb about a block from the address she gave me. I lugged my helmet off and stowed it into a saddlebag and stretched my legs.

I walked the rest of the way, letting my phone direct me until I spotted Madi sitting under a canopy in a little area that had a wrought iron fence. I made a beeline for her, not even caring about the restaurant that she had picked out. She was sitting by herself at little metal dinette set, looking as cute as ever. She looked like she did the last two times I'd seen her; someone that tried to blend in and downplay their beauty. Her brown hair was pulled back from her face, which was covered by thick glasses, and she wore neutral colors. She was someone that was used to being in the background. I stood outside the little gate for maybe five minutes just looking at her before she seemed to notice me. She had a book with her. Instead of doing what everyone else was doing, looking at their phones, she was reading at a book.

"Do they even make books anymore?" I asked myself.

Her eyes shot up to mine and I was blown by how green her eyes were. She looked surprised to see me, and she immediately closed her book and shoved it into her bag. "Yes. They still make books."

I tried to look cool by climbing over the wrought iron gate, and I immediately regretted it. I managed it, but by the time I got to her table I entire left leg was throbbing and the spasms in my back came back with force. I bit my lip to keep from cursing and slowly sat down in the chair.

"Well, I tried to look cool, and I ended up looking like a jackass," I admitted with a wince.

Her brows were drawn up as a sign she seemed to have gathered that I was hurting.

"Um, it would have been impressive if you didn't suddenly look like you pulled an important muscle." She gave a sympathetic smile.

Regardless of the pity, at least I managed to get a smile out of her.

"I wish it was just a muscle I pulled." I shifted in the chair and struggled to get comfortable. "So," I took a breath as I tried to think past the throbbing and pain, "I didn't even pay attention to this place. What kind of food do they offer?"

"It's kind of like an upscale deli, they have great sandwiches and wraps." She eyed me curiously as if she could see me suffering.

"Awesome." I nodded and tried to focus on her. "Your car still running?"

She nodded and offered me her menu. I took it and pretended to scope it out as I tried to think of something to say to this girl.

"So, my occupation is pretty obvious. What do you do? You a lawyer?"

"No." She shook her head as she spoke, her hair not shifting a bit as she did. That was impressive, it was either wound tight, or she had a heavy coat of hairspray. "I'm a paralegal, I work for a law firm that's about two blocks from here."

"So you walked here for lunch?"

She shrugged, looking awkward as she nodded. "It's a pretty day."

"It sure the hell is." I grinned as I spotted a waitress coming our way. "It's a perfect day for a bike ride." Despite the fact that I was in pain slowly edging into agony, I kept on. "If you'd like to go for a ride after work I'd love to take you around town on my bike."

Her eyes went wide, and her mouth dropped open for a second. I didn't know if she was even thinking about the idea. I shifted forward to lean against the table waiting for her to say something. The waitress didn't give us the chance to explore the conversation.

"Hey there," the waitress said as she gave me the once-over. "You guys know what you want?"

I nodded towards Madi, "Ladies first."

That wasn't just a matter of being polite, it was more along the lines of not having a clue as to what I wanted. So, I'd play it cool and order what Madi ordered.

She didn't bat an eye when I did. As soon as the waitress left us, I shifted around in the metal chair again.

"So, about that ride?" I grinned at her to see if she'd bite.

"Motorcycles are dangerous." She looked away from me and seemed to struggle with an excuse. I knew at the first look that she wasn't that kind of girl, but most chicks had a wild side. Maybe this one did, too. "Over four thousand people die in motorcycle accidents each year." She looked at me then, a seriousness in her green eyes, and it almost looked like she was worried about me. "You're not going to turn into a statistic, are you? Are you a part of a motorcycle gang? That does explain all the tattoos." Now I got the feeling she was talking less to me and more to herself. "I can't get caught up with someone that does illegal things."

I cleared my throat to get her attention.

"The key to avoiding a wreck is paying attention, because nine times out of ten, the guy driving a car isn't. Wear a helmet and have a good life insurance policy, it's the best I can do." I shrugged, not trying to make it nonchalant but being in an accident wasn't something I worried about. "I'm not in a gang. They're called clubs, so you know. The tattoos... well," I gave her another cheesy grin and twisted one arm so she could look at the sleeve, "once you get one you have to get more. Then, eventually, you end up covered."

"So, that bar you were at was a motorcycle club?" She looked doubtful, like she expected me to be some kind of gang banger. I never thought I looked the part.

I shook my head, amused. "Yea, but probably not how you think it is. We're all veterans and retirees. So everybody there served in the military in one way or another. It's more of a support group and less illegal shit."

"Oh." Something about admitting what the Brotherhood was about seemed to have eased some discomfort with her. She relaxed in her seat, and I could see curiosity evident on her face. I had her full attention, now. "So you served?"

"Yep." I did a mock salute, hoping that it wouldn't make this a serious conversation. "Nine years and two combat tours in Iraq as an Army engine mechanic."

"That's why you want to look at my car?" Clarity was on her expression as she studied me.

"Well, it was more along the lines of there being a pretty girl driving a car that sounded rough." I didn't see a reason to beat around the bush. Maybe if I made my interest obvious, it would help my chances. "I figured if I did some work on your car maybe that'd give you reason enough to want to hang around with me. Maybe one day I might talk you onto the back of my bike and get you for keeps." I gave her a wink.

She flushed and cupped one cheek as if she could cover it.

"I'm not pretty, and I'm definitely not the kind of girl to get on the back of a motorcycle." she looked away. "As long as that's not a deciding factor I don't see why we couldn't 'hang out' as you put it."

"Not a deciding factor," I assured her. "But I gotta say, you don't know what you're missing. There's something special about being on a bike."

The waitress came back with our lunch, rudely interrupting my pitch. We both ordered wraps, which was something I wouldn't usually go for, but I'm a man that'd eat just about anything you'd put in front of him. It's something the Army teaches you, you don't turn your nose up at unfamiliar food because it could always be worse.

"I'll take it into consideration," she said lightly before she began to eat.

I followed suit, and while our conversation had cooled, we managed to get a little more small talk between bites. Madi was my opposite to an extreme. She was quiet and shy, while I was a man that didn't have a problem saying what was on his mind. She worked hard, but it was from behind a desk. The last time I sat at a desk was in boot camp, and I was far from quiet and shy. But there was something about her that drew me in like a moth to a flame.

"So, there's not a lot of room for parking for your car at the club, but I can do some arranging and fit you in enough so I can get a good look under the hood." I wiped my hands off then went about making sure I didn't make a mess on my face. "Just ride over after you get off."

She nodded and set down the rest of her wrap. "How do I pay you for the work you're doing for me?"

Normally, if someone out of the club was going to get me to do work on their car or shit, I'd ask for payment. Ask for money or get taken advantage of is my usual motto. However this girl didn't really strike me as the type to take advantage, so I shrugged. "Cook me dinner, lemme take you for a ride, give me a call or a text here and there."

"You're making it sound like you want to date me in exchange for fixing my car." She raised an eyebrow.

I chuckled. "I said that before. Only instead of saying date, I said hang out."

"Oh." She faltered a little, looking confused. "I thought that meant you wanted to be friends." I saw her swallow as she considered something. "Do you really think we'll have enough in common to be able to actually date? Like a relationship would work between us?"

"Never heard the saying opposites attract?"

"So, you're attracted to me. You've called me pretty and Sweetcheeks." She was glaring at me now. "But appearance isn't everything. You can't expect a relationship to work just because you find each other attractive."

"Naw," I waved a hand, "it's more than that. It's not the deciding factor, but if you're not going to give me a chance simply because I find you attractive, it seems kind of unfair. Are you trying to brush me off because you have a boyfriend?"

"No." Her voice sounded small, and she looked down into her lap. "It's been a long time since I actually dated someone."

"Really?" I raised both my eyebrows. "Well, that aside. Don't you want to see what it could be like between us? Have a little fun, maybe?"

"You look like the kind of guy that takes advantage of women and breaks their hearts." She looked up at me now. I didn't know if she was serious or not. "If I agree to date you, how do I know that you're not just going to use me and then dump me when you're done?"

"I don't know if that's a compliment," I huffed. I folded my arms onto the table and leaned forward. "How about we make a deal here? I promise not to break your heart if you promise not to break mine?"

"How would that work?" She looked intrigued.

"I'm a one-woman kind of man." I tilted my head a little. "You agree to be a one-man kind of woman, and I think it could work out."

"That's something that goes without saying," she said with a frown. "How else does this work?"

I shrugged a shoulder. "How about you let me come over to your house this Saturday and I show you?"

"We just met, and I'm not having sex with you," she said with a sense of finality.

I chuckled. If I was going to arrange something like that it would take some work and effort to make sure I could get it up and ready for that. I knew it would take some planning. She didn't know that though and I shook my head.

"Not what I was implying. We're out here in the open for all to see. You're not going to cuddle up to me in a restaurant. Let me come over, and we can watch a movie. Let me get close to you and we'll figure it out together. I'll be a good boy and keep it in my pants." I raised a hand like I was a Boy Scout. "I promise."

"You mentioned earlier that you wanted me to cook you dinner." She seemed to be caving... I had her interested. "I guess I could do that Saturday. Do ... do you want anything in particular?"

"I spent a long time eating crap food provided by the military." I smiled at her. "Cook whatever you want, I bet it'll be delicious."

"You're easy to please?"

"Yep." I shrugged. "Doesn't take much to make me happy. What about you?"

She shrugged, too, pulling out her wallet after the check was brought to the table. "A good book with a cup of coffee and I'm happy."

"I will remember that." I plucked up the check the waitress had dropped and eyed it with a grimace. It wasn't too bad, the food was alright, but I wouldn't have guessed it would have been twenty-five dollars worth though.

"I thought I was buying lunch," she protested as I got my wallet out.

"What the hell kind of boyfriend do I look like?" I put one of the hundreds that Jimmy gave me earlier into the little book. "Already said I wasn't going to take advantage of you then dump you. That shit starts now, Darlin'."

She flushed. "Does that mean you're my boyfriend now?"

"I'd like to be, if you're offering." I couldn't help but wink at her.

She floundered for a moment, mouth opening then closing without saying anything. That blush was pretty on her, and I found myself wondering just what else I could do to get her to look like that. Surprisingly, my pants became tight, and I even looked down to confirm that despite the pins and needles in my leg and the throb of my back, I'd still managed to get it up. This chick was magic.

"I guess…" she stood, and I managed to get up to follow. We hadn't gotten our change yet, so I was gonna hang back a bit. "I guess I could be okay with that. I've got to get back to work though, or I'll be late."

I nodded. "Sid, by the way. I dunno if I mentioned it before." I shifted closer to her. "You need anything you got my number. You know what I mean by anything, right?"

I got a nod and she suffered from a bout of bashfulness. I was pushing it, but I wanted to kiss her. I reigned it in and went with just brushing my lips against her cheek. I think I had the same effect on her that she had on me because she looked up at me with those big green eyes and leaned forward to brush a kiss on my cheek in return.

"I'll see you when I get off work." Her voice was soft, and uncertainty was there. I was pretty sure she liked me.

"I'll be looking forward to it." I stayed standing as she walked to the little gate that opened up to the outdoor eating area.

She gave me a few glances over her shoulder as she trekked back to work. I sat back down to wait for my change and watched her until she disappeared. She probably didn't realize it, but she already had my undivided attention.

4

I got back to the club to see Jimmy and another guy unloading what looked like a piece of shit off of a trailer into the yard. I sat on my bike and watched them work, trying not to voice my disgust. I couldn't tell the make of the bike, but it looked like it had been more than dropped. It looked like someone had taken the damn thing through the ringer.

"You know I don't do body work, right? I just do shit with the engines."

"Yea, yea." Jimmy and his friend stopped with the bike in the middle of the damn lot. "All you gotta do is fix the engine."

"I got a friend that'll help with the bodywork," the unnamed man said in response. "I know it looks like a lot of work, but I think once it's running at least it'll be worth the effort."

I carefully eased in around the truck and trailer. I was going to have to set my bike up somewhere else because my usual spot was occupied. I went to the side of the building before I got up and put my bike on its kickstand.

"Where did you find it?" I asked with a frown.

"In a rotted out shed." He shrugged and offered me a hand. "Anthony. Jimmy said you were a wizard with engines and you were the man to see if I wanted to get it running again." He patted the molded leather seat with a hand, and I could already see the guy had big dreams in mind for the bike. "You think you can handle it?"

I took his offered hand and gave it a shake.

"Sid. I can check out the engine but we'll have to see if we can get it started to see how bad it is." I looked at Jimmy. "Go get some gas, would ya?"

With that, we started work. The Anthony guy hung around as we tried to crank the thing up and failed. I wasn't looking forward to doing a whole engine rebuild, but it looked like that was what I was going to do. The next few hours were spent with me sitting on a tarp and working on piecing out this fucked up engine. I lost track of time and the company I had as I worked. It was just something I did. I would get wrist deep in oil and forget anybody else was there.

It was dark when the stuttering rumble of Madi's car rolled into the lot. I had forgotten to clear her out a space with the work I was doing, and I immediately felt like an ass. I set down the part I was working on cleaning out and I stood with some effort. The pins and needles had shifted to outright numbness; as bad as it sounds it was something of a relief. When she got out of the car, I couldn't explain how or why I was happy to see her.

"Hey!" I started wiping my hands clean on my jeans and shirt, not caring about the fact that I was making a bigger mess, as I sauntered over to see her.

She got out of the car, though she kept it running, and looked around the loaded lot.

"So, there's not a lot of room to park my car." She looked at me. "Maybe this isn't a good idea."

"Second thoughts already?" I raised an eyebrow. "Are they about me or are they about me working on your car?"

"Both?" She threw her attention to the rest of the lot then back to me. "It's also getting dark. How are you going to be able to see what the problem is?"

"Lights, baby, they have 'em so you can work at night. Pop the hood, but don't turn it off."

I didn't bother trying to get close to her. I was a mess. I had wanted to see if she'd let me steal some sugar, but if she was going to have second thoughts, I might not want to press my luck. She did as I asked and I hefted the hood up. There weren't any burning smells that I could detect it was just the noise.

"Turn it off," I instructed, and I then patiently waited for her to kill the engine. I gave it a beat to cool before I start checking fluid levels. "When was the last time you had the oil and filters changed?"

When she didn't answer, I looked up to find her fidgeting next to me. She looked embarrassed. "Maybe a few years ago?"

"So," since she was close to me I gave her a nudge. There was a temptation to throw my arm around her, but I was more than a little grubby. "That might create issues. Get me a couple of cartons of oil and an oil filter for Saturday and I'll come over. You'll need to text me your address, and then I'll take care of your problem. We can take a ride after and see if that was the issue."

She nodded as she listened, looking at the engine with me. I watched her pull her phone out then and go the extra measure to text me. My phone vibrated in my pocket.

"You're probably looking at about twenty bucks for all of that," I informed her. "That okay?"

"You are busy." She turned away to look at the mess of a bike I was fucking around with.

"This is what I do," I nodded. I grimaced and looked at her. "You gonna tell me you got something against greasy hands?"

She smiled when she looked up at me. Her face was flushed and she took a step closer so when she spoke it was low. "I don't. I guess I just didn't know what you did, so I assumed you stayed here all day and drank beer."

I put a hand to my stomach. Ya, it was flat; I worked out. The physical therapist emphasized the importance of remaining active as I recovered from my injuries.

"Do I look like I got a beer gut?"

She took the time to look me up and down. It was probably the first time she really looked at me, and I suddenly saw something other than fear or embarrassment on her face. She looked like she liked what she saw. I threw my arm around her now, pulling her so that she was against my side.

"No." She blushed when she looked up at me. Her hand came to pat my stomach and it paused as if she tried to assess just what I was packing. "I guess you don't," she admitted.

"Well, you go and say something like that now I gotta do something like this." I tipped her face up with my free hand and leaned down to catch her lips with mine. I restrained myself enough to not overwhelm her and kissed her gently. I held back the desire to taste her, so I didn't go shoving my tongue in her mouth.

She didn't push me away, she didn't pull back. She tensed and the hand that had been on my stomach fisted my shirt. I kept it brief and chaste, though even with just the brush of her lips against mine I knew I wanted more.

"Okay?" I had to make sure that I hadn't crossed a line and made her uncomfortable.

She nodded, not at all looking embarrassed but instead like she might've liked the fact that I kissed her.

"I'll see you Saturday?" She confirmed.

Yea, I had her attention now like she had mine. I nodded, considered kissing her again, but I pulled away. We had an audience, after all, and I wasn't going to do anything dumb to wreck my chances with this girl.

"I'll be there. Remember, oil and oil filter. I'll come by early so I can get to work."

She nodded and went to get into her car, I cleaned up the small mess I had made and closed the hood. I watched her pull out, not bothering with Jimmy and his friend until she was out of the lot. I had a day to wait but already I was antsy for Saturday.

5

I spent all of Friday trying to work on that damn bike Jimmy brought me. It was a mess that held up my entire day. I shouldn't bitch because it was money that I could use plus something to occupy my time, but it was a bigger pain in the ass than keeping Wilson's bike running. I was in a hurry though, I wanted the damn thing running and out of my way, so it didn't fuck with the rest of my weekend. But, it was damn near ten before we got the bike to successfully crank. Jimmy spent the majority of the time working on it with me. Though he mostly did running for parts and whenever my aches got too much, he'd bring me water and my pills.

"I got some good stuff," his friend, Anthony, said to me when I was aching and pretty much stuck on my ass. "Percocets, they're good for pain."

"Can't." I didn't even look at the idea. But I figured out then that this guy and Jimmy were probably running something more serious than the weed that Teddy and Wilson dealt.

"You're helping me out man," he said in response. "I'd cut you a good deal to help you out."

"I get drugged tested once a month." I looked up at him then. "I test positive for anything that I'm not prescribed, and I get in a shit ton of trouble."

"Fucker's on disability," Jimmy said from behind me. He tossed me a bottle of water with my bottle of pills. "He can get away with smoking pot here and there, but anything else they'll stop paying him for being a bump on a log."

"This bump on a log did more than you did, Chair Force." I didn't pause from working the bottle open and popping pills into my mouth. I chugged the bottle of water down then.

"It's a pity you guys don't let civilians in." Anthony rolled a shoulder. "I could sure help you guys out with business. Get some serious income for guys like you." he nodded at me. "I don't imagine that disability pays much."

"I got a roof over my head, food to eat, and a bike to ride." I gestured for a hand up and with a little effort was hefted to my feet by the both of them. "That's all a guy needs."

"Plus a little pussy never hurts." Jimmy gave my arm a punch. "When you're done with that girl lemme know. I'd like to give her a ride."

"Fuck off, Chair Force." I shook out my numb leg and looked at Anthony. "It'll run now. You just need to clean the rest of that shit up. You're probably going to need a whole new gas tank, though. You're gonna want to get that before you try taking it for a ride."

"I buy one and bring it here you'll put it on for me?"

I nodded. "Tomorrow I'll be out though so you'll have to wait."

"Thanks." He offered me his hand, and I shook it. Then he pulled into one of those one-armed hugs that were always awkward from strangers. "If you change your mind about the other stuff Jimmy has my number. I'll remember to cut you a deal."

I nodded but didn't comment. There were red flags here. I watched as Jimmy and Anthony loaded up the piece of shit bike into a trailer before he pulled out. When it was just Jimmy and me, I felt the need to reach out to the guy.

"You getting into trouble here?"

"Fuck no." He didn't wait for me as he walked back to the bar. "I'm just making extra money. Not all of us can live off the government."

I stayed outside, my pills in one hand and the bottle of water in the other. I didn't think Teddy and Wilson would be keen on Jimmy making extra money depending on what he was dealing in. A shit storm was brewing, and I hoped to God that guy wasn't going to bring the cops running in here. The club had its front as a way for helping vets, I was proof of that. But to make money, they also trafficked pot and CBD oil to people that could use it, people that needed it for treatment. Hell, I was fairly certain Cindy probably made the edibles. And while all of it would get them long prison sentences, they felt like they were helping people out. Plus, they did all they could to keep me out of it.

I had to think about what to do about my hunch, whether to let it be or bring it up to Teddy. I distracted myself with cleaning up the lot. There was a lot to think about and it would weigh on me the rest of the day.

6

I got to Madi's place by ten, mostly because I didn't want to be an ass and be too early. I was happy to find out she lived in a quiet neighborhood in a little house that seemed appropriate for her. At first, I found myself kind of worried that she lived with her parents. However, I only saw her car and there was no garage. No old man came barging out of the house when I pulled up, my bike announcing my presence. I got up, leaving my bike close to her car, because I had tools in the saddlebags, and went to knock on her door. I hoped I wasn't too early. What if she went out the night before? She didn't look like the partying type, but I could always be wrong.

My nerves got settled when she opened the door and smile at me. She was wearing a simple t-shirt and a pair of what I thought were yoga pants.

"Good morning," she said, she had a cup of coffee in hand. "Do you want some breakfast? Or coffee?"

"I'm good thanks." I nodded towards her driveway. "You got the things I asked you to get?"

"I did." She stepped aside, leaving her door open, and went to fetch a bag that she had left on a small blue couch. The inside of her house looked quaint, cozy; it was apparent quickly that she lived alone. It was clean, but she looked like she catered only to herself. She came back to me with the bag and her keys in hand. "You could've come inside."

I lingered in the doorway. "I will later. But I like to get work done first."

I took the bag and her keys from her and stepped off the small porch. She followed me at a length as I went to her car.

"Do you need help?"

"Nah." I unlocked it then popped the hood. "You're more than welcome to keep me company, though."

She seemed to decide just that, taking the time to help me by getting tools that I asked for and asking questions about what I was doing. We built a good banter, and the more we spoke, the more she seemed to relax. I had just finished putting the oil filter and I was starting to put the fresh oil in when I felt her slim arms come around me from behind.

"Thank you," she said lightly. "Usually my dad did this stuff, but since I moved out, I've been determined to be an adult and do things on my own."

There was something to having her arms around me. I looked at her over a shoulder and didn't make a move about pulling away.

"I don't mind doing man things for you. It's a benefit of getting a boyfriend." I leaned back against her when she didn't let me go. "We don't know that I fixed it until we crank her up. It may need something else. I just figured this was the place to start."

Her nose was against my shoulder, and she looked at me through her glasses. "I just wanted to hug you. See if I would get the same reaction that I did when you kissed me the other day."

That was curious honesty. "Did you get your reaction?"

She looked away from me at some pinpoint on my hole filled shirt. She waited a beat before she nodded which caused her to nuzzle me. I closed my eyes for a second and just enjoyed the feel of her pressed along my back and her arms around my waist.

"What happens now?" she asked softly.

"Well," I didn't move, relaxing against her. There was a pleasantness to this that just warmed right through me, "I intend to get you to take me for a short ride. Maybe we can get some sandwiches for lunch and come back. What do you think?"

"That sounds like a good idea." She hesitated for a second before she let me go. "Do you want me to drive?"

I considered it for a second before shaking my head in agreement.

"You take the wheel, I'll focus on the sound this is making." I gestured to the engine in front of me before closing the hood.

She took us for a short ride, both of us listening closely to the engine. It sounded marginally better, and there didn't seem to be any grinding noises as she shifted gears. I looked into her glove box, looking for her owner's manual. She cleared her throat, and after I found what I was looking for, I caught a look from her.

"Not snooping." I waved the thick book at her. "I was looking to see if you had this and the first place to look is the glove box."

She smirked slightly but didn't say a word. We rode around an hour, pausing to pick up lunch before I directed her to take us back to her place. My back had slowly begun to cramp and I couldn't sit in the car much longer. We got out and I stretched with a grimace. It was a whole lot easier to ride around on a motorcycle than it was to sit in a little car.

"Might do some other little things to it, regular maintenance stuff, to see if that helps and maybe add to its general performance. So it's got a little bit better gas mileage and all that."

"You only have to do what's necessary, just so it doesn't die on me," she said as she got out, reaching back in for her lunch bag.

"Well," I closed my door and used the excuse of leaning against her car as a means to stretch out the cramps, "regular maintenance stuff keeps you from having to go to a mechanic."

"Are you trying to give me an excuse to not see you?" She batted her green eyes at me and I was struck.

I think I might have given her a look she'd been giving me when we first met. I shook my head as I brushed off the shock. "No, no. You already agreed to be my girlfriend. So, if anything, that there is a reason for me to see you more often."

"Can it wait?"

"Probably for a week or two." I eyed her. "Why?"

"Maybe instead of being a mechanic when you hang out with me," she blushed but didn't look away from me, "you can be a boyfriend?"

That warmth I felt in my chest when she hugged me before was back, and it seemed to radiate out to my fingertips.

"I can do that." I smiled at her. "I'd actually like to do that. Let's see about going inside and eating lunch. Then we can do some couples shit, right?"

I came to join her around the car, and we walked up onto the porch, her blush still clinging to her cheeks.

"Yea, but not sex yet." She gave me a hard look. "I just met you."

"I didn't ask for it." I leaned against the door frame as I looked down at her. "Nowhere did I say sex. I said couples shit. That could be taking up mutual interests like starting a book club, taking cooking classes, taking long rides on a motorcycle. That kind of shit."

"Not going to let go of the motorcycle part?"

"Nope." A spasm stopped me, and I straighten as she unlocked the door. "I'll be right there in a sec," I assure her as I started hobbling out to my bike.

"Everything okay?"

I nodded. "I figured since we're talking couples shit and stuff I'd go about the property and mark my territory."

It was a joke, and I waited to see if she would take me seriously.

"Do not piss on trees please." She put her hands on her hips. "It's bad enough I'm going to have the neighbors gossiping about the tattooed guy on a motorcycle. They don't need to add the part about him peeing on everything."

I laughed a little and continued out to my bike.

"I got something in my saddle bag I need," I explained. "I promise to keep it in my pants unless I gotta go to the bathroom."

I got my pills from my bag and shoved the oversized bottles into a pocket, I looked up to see her watching me with a worried look on her face. I guessed it was a good idea to throw on the shit on the table on a first date.

"Let's eat and I'll tell ya bout 'em."

She nodded, and we both went into her house. She directed us to a small dinette set that sat in her homey little kitchen. Everything was simply decorated, and it seemed to be the way she rolled. It made me like her more. That was a deciding factor as she laid out our lunch on the table. I pulled out the two bottles and set them next to my food.

"So I told you I was in the Army." I sat down and watched her do the same. She nodded for me to continue. "I served two tours in Iraq. First one wasn't much to write home about, but the last one caused me to have to be discharged medically. I suffered injuries that damn near paralyzed me. These," I nod towards the bottles, "keep me walking and functional."

"So," she said lightly. "You're not a pill pusher or selling drugs for your motorcycle gang?"

"Club," I corrected. "And no. If I did illegal shit, I'd be in serious trouble. I live off of disability, doing anything illegal could take that away."

"Your injury was that bad?" She paused then, her eyebrows coming together. "When you climbed over the metal fence the other day you didn't hurt yourself? It aggravated the injury you already have? Why did you do it?"

"I dunno if you notice, but guys do stupid shit to get girls' attention all the time. I realized immediately it was stupid, but it was too late to abort mission. I bet it didn't impress you at all." I huffed and picked up the sandwich to take a bite. "You're just letting me hang to fix your car."

She snorted out a laugh then, an actual snort. "Oh, it was impressive. Colored me impressed." She followed my lead to unwrap her own sandwich. "I was surprised that you didn't fall since you had this extreme look of pain on your face. It was impressive that you managed to get to the table and sit down." She sobered then watching me as I ate. "How'd you manage that?"

"I've lived with this for four years, going on five." I swallowed hard. "You get used to the throbbing pain, it doesn't mean it doesn't hurt less. Like if I didn't take this shit," I pointed at the two pill bottles, "I'd be a useless pile on the floor."

"Four years?" She looked at me hard then. "How old are you?"

"Do I look old?" I put my sandwich down to drag my fingers through my beard, getting crumbs out as I did. "I'm thirty. How about you?"

"Quid pro quo?" she asked, her eyes twinkling now. "I'm twenty-six."

"That's from a movie." She was a little younger than I thought. That's okay, the age difference didn't bother me. "That the kind of movies you're into?"

We went back to eating, our small talk giving some insight into our tastes in movies and literature.

"I don't really read a whole lot," I admitted as an answer to a question. "I try not to spend too much time in my head. Books usually cause you to do a lot of introspective stuff, don't they?"

"Some can." She was cleaning up the mess we made for lunch, and I got up to help. "But there's reading for entertainment. You're in your head envisioning the story, like a movie but you're the director."

"Huh." I picked up a sponge at the sink and went to wipe down the table. "That's an idea I didn't consider. You got a book you could recommend for me?" I finished up and dusted off my hands and looked at her.

Madi had an intent look on her face as if she was trying to figure out what to suggest then she ended up shrugging.

"You'd have to do that on your own. I'll read just about anything. But you, you need to figure out what you would be into. Fantasy, science fiction? Horror or suspense?" She suddenly grinned at me. "Romance?"

"I guess I'll have to find a bookstore then." I went to her. "Just not today."

"It takes an effort to keep me out of the bookstore," she admitted. "Why not today? I could go with you!"

She actually looked excited at the prospect, it was endearing. But, I had other things I wanted to do. Reading wasn't one of them.

"Not today. There's this pretty girl that I want. And I want her undivided attention like she's got mine." I drifted close to her, breathing in her clean scent and wanting to wrap her up. She seemed to get where I was going, backing up as I got closer and pressing against the wall. "I have had a very good time today."

"You said I should cook you dinner for working on my car," she started to argue. "You're not going to leave now, are you?"

Butterflies kicked up in my stomach, she wanted me to stay.

"Nope. Not going anywhere." I leaned down a little, hovering over her. "I just had something I wanted to do."

"What?" Her eyes were shifting between mine and my mouth.

That was open invitation enough, right? I used one hand to tip her head back, and I closed the distance between us to give her a slow, gentle kiss. It had to be slow, I wanted her to grow on me. If I kissed her like I was desperate to get into her pants, I wouldn't get anywhere. She wasn't ready for that shit, yet. When she started kissing me like that, then I'd be able to throw restraint aside. Now though, I had to be careful because this was new. I didn't want this to go anywhere and I wanted her to trust the fact that I wasn't going to hurt her or her feelings.

I gave her slow, open-mouthed kisses; pulling her bottom lip between mine and sucking lightly before tracing it with my tongue. I didn't prompt her to open for me, she did so on her own. Her hands found my waist and she held on as she reached out to taste me. Her little tongue tip passed my lips, and she took control of the kiss quicker than I was prepared for. I tangled my hand into her ponytail, holding onto the back of her head to keep her close. It was a trade in dominance, I didn't want to overpower her, and there was something about just letting her explore. Give and take, if you will. Like I was showing her the way and she enjoyed it enough that she took over when she wanted.

She pulled me closer, tugging me so that the length of me was pressed against her. She'd feel my erection. I'd spent more time with a hard-on around this girl than I had in the past four years. Reason enough to be intrigued. I pulled back for a breath and felt her panting against me.

"Didn't expect it to go like that," I had to admit.

She shook her head. "Why'd you stop?"

That had me snickering, and I opened my eyes to meet her gaze. "We gotta breathe at some point, baby. If you want more all you gotta do is say so."

"I want more," she breathed, and she was arching up onto her tiptoes to kiss me again.

The kisses were becoming more heated and she seemed to have this desire to touch and explore me, her hands tracing up my chest and toying with my beard. The throbbing of an unpleasant variety began, I think because of the angle I was standing at. I needed relief. I needed to sit down. I pulled away, and she made a soft noise of protest, I didn't give her time to over think it. I tugged her into the living room and found the couch. I sat on it heavily and pulled her down to me. I pulled her against my side and caught her mouth. The pain hadn't taken away that growing hunger I had for her. She kissed me with equal fever, her hands going back to my chest and mapping it out through my shirt. I could only imagine what would happen when she really got going.

I decided to chance it, pulling away from her mouth and tracing the path along her jaw to her throat with my teeth and tongue. Her breaths came out in gasps in my ear, she didn't try to stop me or pull away. If anything she encouraged me, her hands went up to my shoulders and into my hair. As soon as her nails scraped along my scalp, it was like a button was pushed. I tugged her into my lap, pulling her flush against me, so she felt the hardness of my dick between her thighs. I might've growled, I dunno, heat of the moment. I cupped a breast, feeling her fill my palm and wanting nothing more than to paw it out of her shirt and bra to feel skin on skin. I got no protests, only gasps and low moans of encouragement as I pulled my mouth along the length of her neck.

I made the mistake of letting go of her hips because it wasn't long after I started exploring her that her hips started shifting and rolling against me. She was riding me through our clothes, pressing down and making it clear that it felt good to do it. We were dry humping like teenagers. I didn't even bother to stop her; if anything I was just as caught up in it as she was.

"Can I pull your shirt up?" I whispered, not wanting to break whatever spell I had cast on her.

I got a nod, it seemed like it wasn't enough to distract her. I tugged her shirt up, not trying to remove it but get it out of my way. I exposed the lacy white bra under it and tugged the shirt up to her collar. I wanted to taste every inch of her. I didn't ask for permission when I pressed my face between her breasts, I just took advantage of the situation. I tongued every inch of her exposed chest until the bra went from a pretty covering to a wrap blocking what I wanted most. I shoved it up out of my way and latched on the first nipple that became exposed. Her gasps had turned into a moan, and the arching of her hips seemed to have stalled as I suckled on her. I decided to up my ante by cupping one cheek of her ass as I drifted to her other breast to give it equal attention. I felt evident dampness on her pants and if that's not a sign of attraction then I don't know what is. I slid my hand around to help her along, because as fun as it was to have her thrusting against me, I didn't feel like hanging the rest of the night with pants full of crusty cum.

Do I put my hand in her pants or not? I had a mouth full of tits, why not?

The pants she wore didn't cling, and I had my hand in them in a matter of seconds. Either she didn't notice, or she was so caught up with what I was doing with my mouth that she didn't care. I cupped her bare heat in my palm, brushing the bush I felt there with the heel of my hand. It seemed to catch her attention because she gasped in my ear.

"What're you doing?"

I let go of her nipple and pulled away so I could see her face. "Gonna make you cum."

"We're not having sex." Her voice was breathy, and it sounded like she was struggling to be stern.

"Nope," I agreed. "We're not." I swept my fingers along her entrance, teasing her. "But I can make you cum without getting you undressed." Her eyes fluttered, and her hips shifted against my hand. "Do you want me to stop?"

She took in a breath to answer just as I found the magic button she stuttered out, "D-don't stop."

I tried not to laugh, biting my lip as I watched her expression. I circled her clit with my thumb and very carefully eased a finger into her opening. Her eyes closed and her brows drew together as I did, that was encouragement enough. I fucked her shallowly with my fingers, feeling her muscles clench around me each time I pressed into her.

"Do you like that?"

Her breath hitched, and she nodded, her hands still tangled in my hair.

"No sex," I reminded her. "But anytime you want to do this," I hissed at her as I worked another finger into her, "I will until you're ready for full-on sex."

She let out a low whine, and I could feel her cunt throbbing in my hand. She was so close.

"I want you," she choked out, it was a whisper that I was sure I probably wasn't supposed to hear.

"Next time." I arched up and went from circling her clit to just swiping over it back and forth, trying to push her over that edge. "Next time we do something like this, I'm going to strip you down," I growled into her ear. "I'm going to spread you out and lick this sweet little pussy until you're screaming my name. Do you hear me?" She gasped out, trembling as she clung to me. "You want that?" She nodded, I think I pushed her to the point where she couldn't speak. "When you cum, and I know you're close,

I want you to say my name." I pressed my lips to her ear. "What's my name, baby? Say it."

It was damn near a beg from me.

Her arms came around my neck, and she squeezed me hard. "Sid." It was a gasp, and as I curled my thrusting fingers into her, I felt her tense up. "Sid!"

She didn't gush into my hand, she melted still throbbing. She relaxed against me, hanging on and feeling good.

"You like that?" She nodded without answering, probably trying to piece herself back together. "So does that help me keep my boyfriend status?"

She trembled against me as she laughed. I pulled my hand from her pants and was a little disappointed, I would have liked to do more, but I knew better than to push my luck.

"I didn't mean for that to go so far," she murmured against me.

"My fault." I tugged her bra back into place then pulled her shirt down. It was a pity, but I knew we were done fooling around. "I got handsy," I admitted.

"It felt good," she sighed, resting on me.

"I aim to please." I nuzzled her cheek. "I'll make sure I make you feel good every time, deal?"

"That how you plan on keeping your boyfriend claim?"

"If it's necessary," I grinned, "I'll be okay with it."

She untangled herself from me, much to my disappointment, and stood on shaky legs. "I need to get dinner started. I didn't forget about it."

I stood, too, adjusting my erection and stretching out my numb leg. "What's for dinner? I can probably help."

"I was going to do some alfredo with chicken and noodles. That alright?"

"If I could get down on my knee I would ask to upgrade my title of boyfriend to something more serious. If you're going to cook me Italian food and it's good..." I'm a man that's easy to please. But there are just some foods that I can't resist. "If you got any hopes of getting rid of me you're not gonna. That's just going to keep me on you like glue."

She led the way into the kitchen. "I'll remember that."

7

Being with this chick was like being on cloud fucking nine. After that Saturday, she made an effort to call me and text. She would swing by the club after she got off work and we would just hang out. She would watch me work on bikes taking up Jimmy's job of handing me tools while he would go on runs for parts. She warmed up to the bears that frequently hung out at the bar. And by bears, I meant the hairy ass bikers. On Tuesday, I had talked her into staying for dinner and she even ended up back in the kitchen helping Cindy out.

The woman knows how to cook, too. After Saturday, I gave her a serious look. "You ever make lasagna, I will have to put a ring on it and you'll be stuck with me forever."

"You're saying that like it's a threat." She stood beside me at the sink. "I'm beginning to think that I was crazy for being scared of you."

"You were scared of me?"

"You're not a barrel like Mister Tillman," she said lightly as she dried, I cleaned because that's how my mama taught me. "Your tattoos and beard make you look like you're trying to be a bad boy. I see through it now."

"Never judge a book by its cover," I chided.

That night I hadn't tried anything else, I kept my hands to myself and ended it with a chaste kiss. I wanted her wanting me so I behaved myself. I made sure I did that every time I saw her when she paid me a visit. Granted, it was obvious there was something going on. I just wanted to be respectful to her. I wanted her to be for keeps.

Unfortunately on Wednesday, she got to see me on a low. It started raining that morning after I rolled in and it just kept raining. At six when Madi rolled in, I was in agony. I had my TENS unit taped to my back, and I had taken my pills, so I was struggling to get out of the fog of pain that I was drowning in. Rain did this to me. There was something about the dampness that aggravated my damaged nerves and left me crying. I wasn't even aware of her until I felt her cool hands on the back of my neck.

"Are you okay?"

I didn't nod or shake my head, it was something in between.

"His dumbass got out in this weather." I heard Cindy's graveled voice. "The weather messes with his nerves and makes it hard for him to function. He's been like this the majority of the day."

Not a lie, but it was a bit embarrassing to hear her tell the girl I had just started seeing this, not to mention having her witness it.

"Can I help? Tell me how I can help," she asked me, though I only waved a hand in the air. Really there wasn't a lot to do about it.

"Take him home, put him in a hot shower and to bed," Cindy instructed.

"Okay." Madi turned back to me. "How do I get this stuff off his back?"

"Here." The TENS unit was switched off and they pulled the sticky patches off. "Someone help her get him to her car," Cindy belted out like a drill sergeant.

I don't even think the woman served, but the way she shoved these men around, it made me question it. Thick arms hefted me up, and I was set on my feet.

"Can you walk?" It was Teddy.

I gave a nod and walked with his support. My left leg felt like it had a bit of drag to it. There was a downpour outside that no biker in his right mind would try to ride in. The lot was empty and Madi had actually been able to park in what one might consider a parking space. We went out in it, getting soaked, and I was eased slowly into her front seat.

"You need to call your doctor about this shit," Teddy growled at me. "You being an invalid every time it rains is ridiculous."

I could only shrug my shoulders. I managed to get her seat shoved as far back as it would go. It was bearable enough that the queasiness that had been turning my stomach when I sat in the bar had stilled. She got in and gave me a look before pulling out of the lot. The ride was kind of a blur, I think drugs had finally begun to ease in. Valium was an emergency prescription I managed to get from my PCM for times like this. Things still hurt, but it put me into a frame of mind where I didn't care. I was told to use it when things made it hard to function. It left me feeling drunk, but not really. Had Madi not shown up I would have crashed on a cot that was stashed in the bar for guys to sleep themselves sober. The car eventually stopped, and I looked around.

"I didn't tell you where I lived."

"I brought you to my house." Was all I got.

She helped me out of the car, picking up my bag of pills and my tens unit and we both stumbled to her front door.

"You don't have to take care of me," I protested as she worked on getting the door open. "Not at all what I was looking for when I first hit on you."

"You've already taken care of me." I heard her murmur as she helped me into her home. She closed and locked the door behind us. She kept us moving, even when I expected to be dumped on the couch, but she led us into a little bedroom. "Let me take care of you." It sounded like a demand, but it was muddled by my drugged head. "Let's get you undressed and in the shower," she said as she started tugging up my shirt up.

"You can get me naked, baby," I helped her and sat heavily on the bed so I could work the laces of my combat boots, "but I hate to tell you, in this state I'm not going to be able to put out."

"I'm taking that to mean if you sleep in my bed you'll behave?"

"I'd love to get hard just by hearing you say that," I stood, kicking off my boots, "but the junk don't work right this second."

"Good," she gave me a smile and started on my belt, "you won't take advantage."

My jeans were around my ankles with my boxers and I should've felt self-conscious. No one had seen me in the buff in a while and the majority of my lower half was good and scarred up. She didn't give me the chance to cover up. Aside from her sexy blush, she had a professionalism that would do a nurse proud.

"I'll help you get in the shower."

The shower was cut on, and without direction, I put the heat on full blast. She had a walk in shower that was big enough to fit the both of us. I propped my hands up and turned my back to the shower head so that my skin and aching muscles would absorb the heat. I felt the relief even though the drugs fogged my perception of the pain. I groaned quite a bit.

When the hot water was gone it was cut off and Madi was there with a towel. I was dried off and then I caught the sight of big green eyes behind her glasses.

"Nurse getting a good eye full?" I asked, and her blush spread down to her neck. I put my brow to hers as she was helping back into my boxers. "Just so you know," I said as evenly as I could, "I will kick myself for this later for not copping a feel or something."

She laughed and cupped my face. "If your stuff worked I would probably let you take advantage, Sid. I had no idea you looked... looked so good."

"Hardly." She walked me to the bed. "Pick a side Sweetcheeks. Once I go down, I'm not moving."

"I'll let you take the side closest to the bathroom. Here." She brought me to the side she was talking about, and slowly I managed to get on the bed. "Do you want the thing you had on you before?"

"Naw, naw." I relaxed on the world's most comfortable mattress. The bed sheets were soft, and they smelled so good. She tucked me in, and I knew I needed a ring to put on this girl. I felt her lips brush against my temple before I was down for the count.

8

I woke up on my left side, facing a door that was slightly ajar on an unfamiliar white wall. It was warm, and I was covered in a sheet that was a pastel blue with a comforter that had roses stitched into it. The aches and throbbing were still there and I could hear the patter of rain on the window that was above my head. But it felt like the pain was sleeping like I had been. I would have gladly dozed back off if my bladder hadn't been screaming. I sat up and groaned because as soon as I was upright the pins and needles, throbbing, and aching hit me full force. I just had to make it to the bathroom to piss. I didn't want to piss myself in an unfamiliar place. I managed to get to my feet and hobbled into the bathroom. I did my business and noted the state of the bathroom. It was obviously a woman's house, I definitely wasn't home. Did Madi really bring me to her place?

I wandered back into the bedroom to see her stretched out on the other side of the bed. She wore a t-shirt and as far as I could tell that was it save a pair of white lacy panties. I didn't wake up with morning wood, but the picture before me was enough to get my ole' friends attention, despite the aches I had. I glanced down... he must really like her to stand up despite all this shit.

Madi made a noise, bringing my attention back to her, and I hobbled to slip back into bed next to her. I watched her stretch, giving me a great view of her lethal little form. Yea, I had to admit I liked her as much as my cock did. She shifted closer and curled up against my side. I wouldn't have pegged her as a cuddler, but here she was getting all snug against me.

I curled my fingers through the tangled hair the obscured her face then traced a line down her cheek. She took care of me while I was having a bad day, something that occurred on occasion. I had joked about putting a ring on it before, but if she brought me to her bed without an afterthought about me overstepping boundaries that she wasn't ready to cross, there was something here. This was more than sexual attraction. My chest felt tight as I continued to look at her. I don't want to think about the L word… the big L word. But it was there, on the tip of my tongue just looking at her. Fuck, I had fallen full head over heels for her in just this short amount of time. I looked up at the ceiling, watching the slow spin of the fan.

What do I do about this? Do I say something? Do I swallow it and wait? Would it scare her off? The thought scared the shit out of me. *What do I do if she doesn't love me back?*

I didn't get to dwell on my fears long; a hand brushed against my cheek, and I looked to her. Her green eyes were sleepy but beautiful.

"Do you hurt?" she asked.

"Not yet." I swallowed, still feeling the tightness in my chest. "I'll need to take some medicine soon or it'll start up." The word was on the tip of my tongue, lodged in my throat and it was ready to come spilling out like the word vomit it would be. I had to stop it, I didn't want to face the fact that she might reject me. "Don't you have work?"

She got up, affording me a look at her ass and the length of her bare legs and left the room. I decided I'd just stay in bed and see if she'd come back. If I got up, the pins and needles would become more intense and I didn't want to stumble around her house in my underwear.

"I called in sick," she came back with my medicine bag, my TENS unit, and a glass of water. "I was considering calling in tomorrow, too. I want to look at the forecast first before I do something like that."

She offered me my bag and sat beside me on the bed, a glass of water in hand and the TENS unit on her lap. Someone was on nurse duty. I sat up a little bit and I began to dig into my bag. Nerve pills first; I popped two in my mouth without a thought and took the glass to drink them down.

"Don't get yourself fired on my account." I looked at her, that word still hovering in the forefront of my mind. "I'm not worth you losing your job for."

"I haven't taken a vacation since I started the job." She smiled at me. "I have been sick maybe two days over the last three years. Nobody can get mad at me for calling in today and tomorrow," she said and looked sure of it, too.

I sat the bag on the bedside table and she did the same with the glass of water and the TENS unit.

"Before I met you," she started, "I would go to work and come home. I didn't do anything outside of my routine. I didn't have fun, I didn't think about men outside of fantasizing about celebrities that I would never meet." She paused, looking away from me as she seemed to think about what she was about to say. "I met you, and now I want to go out. I have fun with you. Even if it's just hanging out at that bar or if we come back here to watch a movie. I feel like you've given me the desire and motivation to live."

"Motivation to take a ride on the back of my bike?" I playfully prodded.

She let out a laugh and her eyes connected with mine again. "Not yet, but I imagine you'll probably wear me down eventually."

I picked up her hand from where it rested on her thigh. "How do I repay you for looking after me?"

"Don't break my heart."

It came out so softly, and it left me choking on that word again. I looked her in the eye as I brought her hand to my lips, kissing her palm. "I won't break your heart, baby," I murmured against her palm. "I want to keep it. It doesn't do me any good to break it."

She leaned into me and kissed me hesitantly, she still seemed unsure at initiating things. I let her decide the intensity of the kiss, the depth. Her hand slipped out of my grip and combed through my beard then up in the mess that was my hair.

"When you say things like that," she pulled away just enough to whisper to me, "it makes me want you more."

My cock twitched just at those words. Damn, had I known this was where I would have ended up yesterday morning I would've come more prepared.

"Tell me something," I tangled both of my hands into her hair, keeping her close, "are you a virgin?"

She flushed, and I got the hint that this wasn't a cool question for me to ask. She pulled out of my grasp and twisted her lips up as she looked at me. "No."

I blinked, not sure why I thought she was. "Something tells me that there is some negativity behind the first time." I watched her carefully, a knot slowly weighing in my gut. There was an inexplicable urge to protect her. That L word was probably the source. "Somebody hurt you?"

"Probably not in the way you think." She started fidgeting with the comforter that covered me, not meeting my gaze. "The guy I gave myself to decided that was all he wanted."

Ah, trust issues. That explained a lot. I sat up, trying not to grimace at the discomfort I felt, and I pressed my brow against hers. I was so close to saying that L word I had to bite my tongue to keep from saying it. When I was sure I wouldn't go blurting it out, I forged ahead.

"I want more from you than just sex. I want you, all of you."

I didn't get the chance to say anything else as she caught my mouth and pressed me back into the bed with an assertiveness that I wouldn't have guessed she had. She leaned over me and kissed me with a hunger that I contributed to the last time we had been alone. Her tongue was in my mouth and her hands were in my hair. When her hands started to wander, I knew that the 'not having sex' thing was probably out the door. I managed to tug away.

"I would very much like to take advantage of this," Even though I was hard, I knew I probably wouldn't last long enough for anything respectable, "but I don't want to be a disappointment."

She had her hands on my chest and were working over the lines of the tattoo there; an eagle with its wings spread and an M16 bared in its claws in the traditional style. There was something about her feather-like touch that had goosebumps breaking out everywhere.

"How would you be a disappointment?"

"I'd probably get a few good thrusts in before I'd lose it and leave you hanging." I had to be honest. "My boy is interested, don't get me wrong. But, he's not dedicated... with how the weather is." I had an idea then, and I reached down to grip her ass. "Wait... what did I say I was going to do the last time I was here?"

"What?" She looked intrigued.

"Take off your panties," I growled at her.

I wanted her, but I knew I wouldn't be able to perform like I wanted. So, there was that alternative.

"Why?" Blush colored her face and she looked excited.

"I said I wanted to spread you out and lick that sweet little pussy until you were screaming my name. I can't spread you out, I need to stay laying down. But you can sit on my face," I said shifting until I lay flat. "And I can still lick you until you're screaming my name."

"Sit on your face?" she asked, suddenly embarrassed.

I nodded and didn't give her the opportunity to argue with me. I tugged her so that she was leaning against my chest, "Ain't gonna hurt me a bit. C'mon. You'll feel good I promise."

I wanted this now. I wanted to know how she tasted. I got looks from her before she slipped her panties off and dropped them on the floor. Then she straddled my chest.

"How do I do this?"

I felt the dampness of her curls on my chest and I couldn't help but groan. I wanted her wrapped around me. My dick throbbed in agreement, but I knew he was a filthy liar.

"Like you are sitting on me now," I explained, "but with your legs on either side of my face."

Her brows drew together, and she shifted until she hovered over my face. I got a good look at her outer lips and the small tuft of hair just above it. I licked my lips and wrapped my arms around her thighs, I didn't give her the chance to protest or adjust, I just dove in with my lips and tongue like a starved man. I heard a startled gasp and I felt the bed shaking; she had grabbed the headboard. I pressed my tongue between her lips and tickled it along her slick opening. She was as responsive as I remembered her to be and she bucked against my face as soon as I started tonguing her clit. That was reason enough to attack the button so I lashed with my tongue then latched my mouth around it. As soon as I start suckling on her, I feel the trembling begin.

Was she that worked up just from kissing me? Maybe it was the talk or the prospect of sex. If she wants me that much, I better give her something.

I released one thigh and found a way to ease a finger into her. She moaned, her hips rolling against my mouth and her muscles clenching around my finger. I released her clit for a breath.

"You taste so good, I could eat you all day." I worked another finger into her, curling the fingers as I thrust them into her. "I can't wait to feel this around my dick."

I latched back onto her again, hearing a whine as I seemed to be driving her closer. It was a whole lot quicker than the last time we were together like this. This time, there was a whole lot less clothing involved. One of her hands dug into my hair, and I heard a short string of "don't stop" coming from her like a prayer. I pressed my fingers against the upper wall inside her, swirling her clit as I sucked in hard. She cried out. It started like a shriek and ended as a drawn-out moan, before she clenched around my fingers hard enough to hurt. I looked up to see her face, her eyes were closed and her brows drawn up. Her mouth was opened as if she was caught off guard, her lips forming a small 'oh.' It was probably the sexiest expression I'd seen her have.

I eased my fingers from her and gave her tentative licks while I watched her face. Her flavor matched her scent, musky with a slightly salty tang. It wasn't something I minded having on my tongue. I was going to clean every bit of wetness from her, but she began to twitch and carefully eased her way off my face. She melted onto the bed beside me, panting lightly as she seemed to come down from the euphoric high I had put her on.

"That was fantastic." I heard her say.

"I am happy to please," I assured her as I rolled on my side to face her though her head was down by my thighs. "So, since you called in what do you intend to do with your day? Just stay in bed?"

"We could take a shower, brush our teeth and all that." She raised an eyebrow at me. "If you're achy we could watch a movie or something."

"Could take me back to my place," I offered.

I found it hard not to touch her; I stroked my hand up her thigh and cupped her bare ass. Damn the rain. All that was between her and me was a pair of day-old boxer shorts.

"Are you saying you don't want to stay the night again?"

"Nope. But unless you like the idea of me hanging out around here naked, I'll need some clean clothes," I pointed out, kissing her knee.

She seemed to catch a better look at me because she sat up and started dragging her fingers through my beard.

"You're a mess." That blush came back, and I gathered what had her embarrassed. "Let's get a shower and get cleaned up and then we'll go get you some clean clothes."

She helped me out of bed and the stiffness wasn't just in my pants.

"You going to take a shower with me?" I asked with a groan.

"I was thinking I would do that." She directed me into the shower and I had the pleasure of finally seeing her naked.

I had felt her breasts in my hands, I had my mouth latched onto them about a week ago. But touching and tasting were totally different from seeing. I wanted to bury my face between them as I thrust into her. I was cursing myself because I wouldn't be able to do that, at least not today. She turned on the hot and turned me into the spray so that my hair and beard were wet.

"It bother you that you had my beard all soaked?" I asked as she picked up her shampoo and started to lather up my hair.

I stooped to offer her a better angle. Her fingers tangling in my hair and massaging my scalp was enough to make me want to throw all my cares about embarrassing myself with a poor performance down the drain. Her hands drifted down, and she went about shampooing my damn beard.

"It didn't," she assured me. "I just never had someone do that to me. I didn't expect to see so much... umm... me... left on your face."

"Means I did a good job." I smirked at her.

We traded places so she could rinse me. Liking the idea of cleaning each other, I picked up her shampoo and started lathering up her hair. I didn't get too far though as she slipped down to her knees and caught hold of my erection. I had been sporting it for a short while now, something that frequently happened around her. It hadn't gotten painful yet, but with the way she started stroking me with a surety, that surprised me.

"What're you doing there?"

"Showing you my appreciation," she said before closing her lips around the tip of my cock.

She was giving me the vision I had when I first saw her, her sweet lips wrapped around me. I kept my hands tangled in her hair as she swallowed me.

"You don't have to." I swore, but I made no move to stop her.

Her hand kept working me as she bobbed her head along the length of me. She didn't release me to argue with me, just kept up the work until my hips were thrusting forward of their own accord.

"God, that feels so good."

I tilted my head back into the spray as she brought me closer and closer. I wanted to hold out, feel the deliciousness of her mouth for as long as I could but there was a tightening in my balls and a throb in my dick that was quickly becoming too much. I wavered and I pressed a hand to the tiled wall, groaning build up was becoming too much.

"I'm gonna cum," I managed to choke out.

She didn't stop as if I hadn't warned her at all. If anything she seemed to increase her efforts. Her free hand came to cup and massage my balls.

"God!" I didn't know if it was a plea or a curse, what she was doing to me felt so good.

I halted her movements with the one hand I still had in her hair and I gave a hard thrust forward before I exploded. I saw stars, my vision blacking out. The groan that was torn from me echoed through the room, and it was all I could do to remain standing.

"God," I repeated as sense started to return to me. "Definitely, definitely saving up to put a ring on it."

She stood up, between the wall and me. "Put a ring on it?"

"Yep." When I was sure I wasn't going to fall, I tugged her under the spray before it got too cold so I could rinse her hair. "I keep saying you're stuck with me. I gotta make it official."

"Don't you think you're thinking things like that too soon?" She squirmed.

"Naw," I assured her. "It's gonna take me a while to get a ring to put on it. I think that's enough time to win you over to the idea," I declared, still drunk on the orgasm she gave me.

"Lucky for you," she started as she wrapped her arms around me, "you're cute, and I might actually be susceptible to the idea."

"I hope," I reached behind me to shut off the shower, "I like the idea of having that. C'mon before we get too pruney. If your offer to stay the night is still on the table, I'm going to take you up on it."

I led the way out of the bathroom and reached for the towels we had used the night before.

"Is that…" Her voice cracked a little. "Is that from when you were in Iraq?"

I looked back at her then glanced down, my left side was a mess of scar tissue. It looked like melted skin, it was hard to discern any muscle beneath. I looked at her, afraid of what I might see. I didn't want to face disgust.

"Yea." I swallowed, waiting for any verdict that might smash all this back to reality. "Not a pretty sight, sorry."

She shook her head, taking a towel from me. "It doesn't look pretty. But it's you, and it's not going to keep me from wanting you."

"This," I wrapped the towel around my waist. "Is why I want to put a ring on it." I pulled her to me and wrapped my arms around her. "You worry about me breaking your heart? Do me a favor and promise to not break mine, okay?"

"I promise." She smiled at me.

9

Madi called in sick on Friday, too. I directed her to my sorry excuse for an apartment and watched carefully as I unlocked the door to let her in. While her house might have been small, it fit Madi to a T. My apartment didn't look a bit like me. It looked similar to barracks that I stayed in while serving, only slightly bigger and without a roommate. I left her to explore as I packed a bag. I made sure I had an extra battery and all my meds. While in the bathroom I came across an old box of condoms and looked at one just to see if they were still any good.

Expired. Fuck me.

"What are you doing?" She stood in the doorway. When I looked back at her I saw something else held her attention.

I followed her gaze and saw that she was looking at the shadowbox my mother had made for me when I was going through physical therapy. It had all my ribbons and medals with a picture of me in my dress uniform and in my fatigues.

"Is that you?" She came into the room and went right to it, looking at it intently.

"Yep." I finished packing up my bag and looked at her. "What, you don't like the beard?"

"Sidney Joseph Redding," she murmured instead, seeming to test out the quality of my name. "You got a purple heart," she said looking at me in awe as she pointed at the medal in the shadowbox.

"Yep," I confirmed, not wanting to expand on the circumstances.

"Wow, I didn't realize." She shook her head and looked back at me with her full attention. "This is all that disability will pay for?"

"Mom and dad helped with the furniture. Disability keeps the roof over my head and the lights on. Fortunately, water is included in the rent." I folded my arms over my chest. "You judging me?"

"No, no, God if it seemed like I was, I'm sorry." She started fidgeting with the hem of her shirt like I was giving her a real hard time.

I snorted and came over to her. "That shit was over four years ago. It's been awhile since I even looked at it. If anything, the only time it occurs to me is when I'm down for the count hurting or waiting in line at the VA. Don't worry about it, Sweetcheeks. I'm taken care of."

"If you lived with someone, would it affect the amount you got in disability?"

"Nope, but I'm not really looking for a roomie. Let's get going though." I went to get my bag, throwing it over a shoulder. "I'm ready to get back to our slumber party when you are. If our party is going to include sex of the real kind, I'll need to make a stop by a gas station at least to get some rubbers."

Her face went pink and it was hard for me not to smirk at her. The last bit was said with the intent to embarrass. Kind of an asshole thing to do, but her poking put me on edge a little.

"Would you consider moving in with me?" she squeaked, almost a whisper.

I nearly dropped my bag and I stood there staring at her for what felt like hours, but it could've been five minutes.

"You said earlier that it was too soon for me to think about putting a ring on it. Isn't it too soon to ask this question?"

"It was something I was considering while we were laying in bed earlier," she admitted, and she walked past me like she hadn't just said something important. "I want you to stay the entire weekend with me. Even if we don't do anything and it's just 'couples shit' we talked about a week ago. Then, if we're in agreement to not breaking each other's hearts, we can talk about being roommates seriously."

"Uh huh." I followed her out, watching her closely.

I was growing on her like she was growing on me. If she was talking about me moving in seriously, then I wasn't the only one playing for keeps.

10

The rain came quite late Thursday night while we were sleeping. I had the great pleasure of waking up with only a slight drug-induced haze and Madi wrapped around me like a blanket. Morning wood was up and loaded, too. I twisted and rolled so we were lying chest to chest. Sleeping next to her definitely made the idea of moving in with her even more appealing. She kept her pajamas simple, a t-shirt and whatever panties she had been wearing that day. It gave me the opportunity to feel the silkiness of her thighs and follow them up to the curve of her ass. Heaven, this was where I was. It couldn't get better than this.

I could stay like this all day if it weren't for the need to piss. That's what got me up. I slid out from under her and hurried to the bathroom. After getting finished with business, I went ahead and brushed my teeth. The question here was, do I wake her up or do I just make breakfast?

It's been a day, I think I can manage something, I told myself.

I wandered into the kitchen and raided the fridge; eggs and toast were pretty much my options. Not knowing her well enough as to how she might like her eggs, I opted for scrambled. I was watching the eggs at the stove when I felt her slim arms wrap around my waist.

"You cook?"

"I have a few things that I can cook," I answered. "Don't expect a four-course meal out of me."

I didn't hesitate to lean back against her. I stood there in only a pair of boxers, and when I glanced over my shoulder at her, I confirmed the fact that she hadn't bothered to get dressed either. This seemed domestic.

"I dunno how you like your eggs. Scrambled okay?"

She nodded and just seemed content in holding onto me. It gave me the warm fuzzies. I turned the stove off and plated to the eggs with toast already buttered.

"We gonna eat like this? I'm not sure how we could do this. Got any ideas?"

"Sorry. I enjoy hugging you." She let go of me after giving my ass a slap. "I doubt it would be practical for me to try to eat while hugging you. You're bigger than me, and that would be messy."

She got us two glasses of orange juice and we sat at her table for breakfast. Gave me that domestic feeling again.

"This how shit will be in ten years?" I asked as I took a sip of the brightly colored juice.

"You expect this to last that long?"

"I expect it to last longer, baby." I didn't look at her as I ate. "Gonna put a ring on it, remember?" She didn't argue. Instead, she nodded. "Then that's the way this will be. You going to complain?"

"Nope."

We spent the day being lazy around one another, didn't bother getting dressed and just lounged around. The kind of shit you want to do with your significant other. It was after lunch that things went from just being comfortable, to being frisky. Madi started out with just stroking my thigh then twisting so that she could kiss my neck. I wanted to see where this could go.

Her hand skipped over the growing tent in my shorts and splayed on my stomach to toy with the line of hair that led down. Her fingers skimmed at the waistband before I decided to take some sort of action.

"You really want to do this on the couch? Wouldn't it be a better idea to do this in the bed?"

She waited a bit before getting up and leaving me on the couch. I watched her go into the bedroom, and I knew, fighting a grin, what she wanted. I got up and followed her, my excitement at the prospect of finally having sex after so long was pretty evident. She had the box of condoms out and on the bedside table. When she saw me enter, she didn't wait for me. She tugged her shirt up and over her head, giving me a full view of just how beautiful she was.

"Don't tell me you intend to just stand there and stare at me," she huffed lightly her hands fidgeting with her panties.

"Leave them on," I raised a hand to stop her, "I want to take those off." I saw her eyes widen and I prowled forward. "But I want to just look at you and drink in how fucking gorgeous you are." She shifted, and before insecurities could get the better of her, I cupped her face in both my hands looking her in the eye. "You are fucking gorgeous."

I didn't give her the chance to protest either. I caught her mouth and kissed her with the hunger I felt from the moment I first saw her. I could feel her wanting to get close, to press our bodies together.

I wasn't giving her what she wanted. I turned us and backed her up until she hit the mattress. I left her mouth, tilting her head so that I could work my way down her neck. My hand drifted down to cup a breast. I brushed my thumb around her nipple until I felt it tighten. I started to lean her back until she was resting on the bed. I followed the path my hand had gone until I reached the breast I had been fondling before. I traced the line of her breast with my tongue, teasing the underside until I swirled back around to the peak. I didn't neglect the other breast, teasing the nipple until it tightened too. Her hands were in my hair and they tugged me in the direction of her other breast, encouraging me to pay it equal amounts of attention.

My free hand wormed its way into her panties where I mapped out her slick opening. She was already wet for me and that thought was enough to get me hard. I was ready to dive right in. But this was a part of the build-up, not just for her. I enjoyed the flavor of her skin, the smell of her and her desire, the way that she clenched around my fingers when I pressed them into her, the soft gasps and low moans she made as I gave her pleasure. It all curled through my ears and into my brain… and then right down to my dick. With the way she arched and rolled her hips against my hand, I knew that I wasn't going to be able to wait much longer. I needed to have that sweet heat wrapped around me.

I pulled away from her and used my free hand to get a condom out. Ripping it open with my teeth, I gave the rubber a hard look to make sure it was good to go before I shucked off my boxers and rolled that bad boy on. I pulled my hand from between her thighs and tugged her panties away as I did. I had originally wanted to spread her out and have her cooing like she was while I tasted her, but that plan was tossed out the door. I had wanted this girl so long that I couldn't wait anymore now that she'd given me the go ahead.

"C'mon baby, let's get on the bed right."

She nodded, her face flushed and her eyes dilated. As soon as she was settled in the middle of the bed, I prowled over her and settled down between her thighs. Her breasts pressed against my chest and her arms immediately when around my neck as I went to kiss her. The connection that existed between us seemed to intensify as soon as my cock pressed against her outer lips.

Words bubbled up in me as I started to press into her and all the thoughts that circulated her seemed to well up like a pot ready to boil over. I thrusted forward slowly and the sweet hold started to envelop me, giving under the pressure until I was fully seethed in her hold.

"God," I hissed out against her lips, "you feel so good, baby, so good."

I'm a babbler, I won't lie. Each time I pulled back then thrust back into her was accompanied by me telling her how beautiful she was and how much I loved the feel of her on my cock, not counting the barrier of the condom. I reached down to hitch one thigh over my hip, she didn't need a lot of prompting after that. Her legs wrapped around my waist and I tilted us so that each thrust I made into her brought me deeper and deeper into her.

Muscles spasms started, because of course they would assault me when I was in the middle of fucking a beautiful girl. I grimaced and managed to open my eyes so I could see her expression.

"Not going to be able to go as long as I wanted." I had to break it to her because I either needed to speed this up for us both to have a happy ending or I'd go soft, and that would be embarrassing. I've had it happen before, part of the reason why it's been a while.

Her eyes fluttered open connected with mine, she nodded though it seemed like she was at a loss for words. I slipped a hand between us and started brushing my thumb over her clit, trying to press her along to that orgasm that I could feel squeezing me tighter.

"Don't hold out," I begged. "I can't much longer."

She cried out, her fingernails digging into my back and her cunt clenching around me so hard that I choked out a groan in response. I clenched my eyes closed as my vision started to swim, like I was actually being choked. I saw stars and tensed up as I exploded inside her, well close enough to inside her.

"Fuck!" I curled my arms around her, managing a few more short thrusts before I was milked dry. "Fuck!" It was like a plea being ripped from me. I buried my face against her neck as the feelings shuddered through me. "I fucking love you."

Of course, reality didn't crash back into me and let me know how fucking dumb I was. Not yet. We were both still drunk from sex, and it probably hadn't occurred to her what I said, much less me realizing it. The fact that I had managed to stay hard through the entire thing was saying something. I wanted to stay buried between her thighs and just live here. It felt so good, and it seemed to take so little effort. But, I was sure she wouldn't be able to take my full weight on her for too much longer. Not that I'm fat, two hundred pounds of mostly muscle, thanks.

I turned us on our sides, unhooking her ankles so that I wasn't putting unpleasant pressure on her. Then I relaxed and breathed in the musk that seemed to accompany a good fucking. And that was when reality hit me like a ton of bricks. I tensed and waited for her to react.

Maybe she would ignore it? Did I want her to ignore it? Did I want her to acknowledge it?

Fuck me! I told this girl I loved her! I knew I loved her. I realized it Thursday night while she was nursing me back to health. But, I hadn't planned on blurting it out like that and so soon.

She rested against me, and for a second I thought she might've fallen asleep. I felt for a moment like I dodged a bullet. I wasn't sure if I should be relieved or disappointed though. Regardless, I was still fucking scared. Was I so much of a bitch that I'd tell her I loved her during sex all the time? I couldn't imagine a chick complaining, but if she wasn't ready to hear the words, it might derail our short-lived relationship.

"You love me?" she questioned quietly. So much for her being asleep. "Did you mean that?"

I pulled away from her, swallowing hard as I met her big green eyes. "I uh... I really didn't mean to say that." I released a shaky breath. "But it was said. No point in trying to take it back. Yea," I nodded and started to relax and accept my fate, "I love you."

If her eyes could have gotten any bigger, I would have been surprised. I wasn't sure if I should have been afraid or not. My heart was thundering in my chest and I could barely hear anything past the rush of blood in my ears.

"I'm not ready to say it back to you," she admitted. That wasn't rejection, was it? "I'm not going to kick you out," she said slowly, sensing my fear. "I... I just didn't expect you to get here so soon. I never thought I'd hear a man say that to me."

"Why not?"

It didn't make sense to me why she hadn't heard those words before. She was beautiful and she was loving to me even though she hadn't admitted to loving me. She seemed caring and had been open with me. Surely some jackass was able to see the prize that she was.

"Because," she looked away even though she rested against me, "I didn't think I was good enough."

"That asshole's loss in my gain," I said, and I tilted her chin so she was forced to look at me. "I only curse him for doing this to your self-esteem. If you were still with him, you wouldn't be here with me. Then where would I be?"

I didn't give her the chance to dwell on it, I kissed her slowly to distract her and hoped I hadn't royally fucked myself.

11

Despite my ill-timed admission of love, I hadn't completely tanked my chances with Madi. She didn't send me home; which would have been hard to do seeing how my bike was still parked at the bar. She didn't put me on the couch either. I still had the pleasure of being in her bed, wrapped around her. The first time we had sex wasn't the last time either. On Saturday while we watched a movie, I'd mention the name but I forgot it, she started giving me the signals. She managed to get me up on two occasions, a record I hadn't been able to get back to in four years. I was glad to experiment with how responsive she would be in different positions and seeing how long I could last while thrusting into her from behind and then with her riding me from above. I don't know which she enjoyed more, but the latter seemed to make her more vocal.

I could get used to waking up to her curled into me and being surrounded by her scent. I wanted to wake up like this every day. Come Sunday though, we had to go back to the real world. She had work to get back to and I couldn't keep her with me forever. She took me back to the bar for my bike and we spent the rest of the day around people. People are overrated. Having sex in her bed is a much better idea if you ask me.

"Whipped," Jimmy sang out when I saw her off. "Pussy whipped in under a month. Goddamn, I need to revoke your man card."

"Man if you had the opportunity to get good pussy, you'd be whipped, too." I didn't even pay him any mind. I wasn't offended by what he said.

"I ain't seen you in days." He pulled his wallet out and counted out a few bills. "Ted said you were damn near dead on Wednesday. You telling me you've spent the weekend being balls deep in that?"

"Not giving you details." Though there was some definite satisfaction that I was feeling after my long weekend in Madi's arms and bed.

"That's enough for me." He offered me the money. "From Anthony. He was real happy with the work you did on that bike. He was talking about seeing about making arrangements to start bringing his friend's bikes here; if you're interested in the extra money."

"I ain't getting into illegal crap," I said without looking at him. "And if you're into shit without Teddy or Wilson knowing about it, you could get into serious deep shit."

"Take the money," he snapped. "And worry about your own broke ass." I took the offered money from him and met his glare with one of my own. "Mind your own Goddamn business and you ain't got anything to worry about."

I stuffed the money into my pocket and nodded but it left a sour taste in my mouth. I gave him a dark look before going into the bar. I didn't know what he was dealing in, but the answer was enough to confirm the fact that Teddy and Wilson weren't involved. What kept me from going to them though was the fact I had nothing. I had a hunch and that was it. Maybe a little more than a hunch with what Anthony said to me.

"Hey, Cindy." I wandered into the kitchen, watching her as she cleaned up the mess from dinner.

"Hey pretty boy," she said without even looking at me.

"You gotta minute?" She stopped to look at me, her brows drawn down and her expression telling me I better have some good shit for interrupting her. "I have a hunch that shit is gonna go down. Do I follow it? Do I tell Teddy about it? Or do I keep my nose clean?"

"You're asking me for advice?" She looked surprised, like she didn't expect me to do something like that.

"This is on the basis that you're smarter than me." I figured buttering her up was the best idea. Because there were a few different ways to take this and I hadn't figured out the best way to go about it.

Her lips twisted up to one side, and she gave me a hard look like she didn't take me seriously.

"If you're serious," she started then went back to work at cleaning up the kitchen. I helped by drying whatever she handed me since I was distracted. "You need to ask yourself a few questions. Does it concern the club? If it does then you need to talk to Teddy." She didn't even hesitate with that. "If it doesn't concern the club and this is some kind of shit you've gotten in with that girl, like done something stupid and knock her up, I'm going to cut off your balls and serve them for dinner tomorrow. Madison is too good for you to ruin."

"First," I couldn't keep from sounding insulted, "I wrapped shit up. Second, I don't want to fuck up shit with Madi. That's gold and I know it. I'm not that fucking stupid."

"Well, good." She handed me a heavy skillet that I nearly dropped. "I like her, it's not every day one of you brats bring something good in here. She's not an old lady."

"So you're telling me not to make her my old lady?"

"Are you in that deep, boy?"

I grimaced. If there was anyone that could give me solid advice it was probably Cindy. "I told her I loved her," I admitted, and I couldn't look at her. I knew how much an ass I sounded like. I had only been with the girl for two weeks, and I'd already dropped the L word.

"Wow." She stopped what she was doing, and I knew she was staring at me. "You meant it, too, didn't you?" I still couldn't look at her, but I nodded. What was the point in denying it? "The look on your face, boy. I guess I can see it. She's a sweetheart." She went back to cleaning, "Hold onto her, buddy. If she didn't kick you out on your ass when you said that she probably feels the same."

"Can't just be that I'm good at throwing dick?"

"I doubt it." She took the towel from me. "If you feel like you need validation you're not going to get it here. If your gut is telling you something, you should follow it. Just don't go wrong by that girl, getting too serious too quick might scare her off. Quit being stupid."

"Now you're asking too much." I huffed for show. She and I had a banter going that I couldn't ruin because I felt vulnerable. "I was thinking about getting a ring, I gotta start saving for it now."

"Get your ass out of here if you're not going to listen to me," she commanded and popped me in the ass with the towel.

At first, I didn't think she gave me anything I could use. My gut was telling me something, though. It was time I followed it.

12

I decided that from then on I'd be keeping a closer eye on Jimmy. Unfortunately, for me, Teddy and Wilson had patched Jimmy into the club while I had been enjoying my weekend with Madi. I found it out the hard way when I went to have a talk with them on Monday morning.

"The fuck have you been?" Wilson snapped when I came into sit in front of the desk.

"Wednesday fucked me up. I was down and out for a few days." It wasn't a lie.

"Down and out with that girl?" Teddy asked, because damn him, he saw straight through me.

I shrugged, no point and hiding it. "Yea. You going to rail me for it?"

Wilson snorted and shook his head. Teddy, on the other hand, gave me a nod like he knew that shit I'd been through for the last few years.

"Did you want something?" Teddy asked curiously.

"What're your thoughts on us doing side jobs?"

"Side jobs?" Wilson asked with a raised eyebrow. "Boy, don't you start being stupid on me. You know what you're talking about when you say side job?"

All these people were implying that I was stupid. I grimaced at him and tried to keep it from getting me. I scratched my jaw as I eyed the other man.

"I have my ideas. Though side jobs for me are working on bikes and getting paid under the table. Side jobs for you guys are a little more illegal than tax evasion. But, what I'm asking is, do you monitor the side jobs that we do?"

Teddy's eyes narrowed and I wasn't sure if he caught my meaning or not.

"I don't keep tabs on what you do. Do I need to? Everyone we patch in is vetted to some degree and given six months to see if they're a fit and can be trusted. We do things that aren't legal on a lot of levels. If we had the cops coming in here with the cooking Cindy does and the papers we keep, it wouldn't be hard to tell what we do. Everyone here would do some kind of jail time."

He didn't get my meaning. I rubbed the back of my neck and I found that I was second guessing myself. Had this gotten too dangerous?

"You're only dealing in pot, though, right?"

These were good people, I knew they were. They wouldn't deal real poison to people, would they?

"Quit beating around the bush, Sid," Teddy said with a growl. "You got some accusations to make?"

He didn't look happy with me and I didn't feel like an ass for asking, but there was a growing sense of dread in my gut. I thought Teddy was a good man, I thought Wilson was, too. When they told me that they were getting pot from the closest legal state and trafficking it over to those that used it for medicine and couldn't afford to move, I thought them heroes on some level. But, Jimmy didn't really strike me as a hero; just a dumb kid.

I swallowed as I looked at him and I tried to decide if I wanted to call him on the suspicion I had on Jimmy. But, now with the doubt in my gut, I didn't know if I could stomach looking at Teddy with the knowledge that he dealt in harder substances.

"Is it serious shit, man? I gotta know." I looked to Wilson. "You guys kept me in the dark to protect me. But if it's serious shit, the shit that kills people, I can't be apart of that. And I don't mean just to protect my paycheck."

I still had morals, they had been protected by this man but now they were threatening my view of him.

"We don't," Wilson started as I looked at him. "We don't do anything that will cause any of the people we deal with harm. You know what Cindy is cooking, you're in the kitchen up her ass as much as the rest of us are. Why are you asking questions?" He didn't look offended like Teddy did, his expression was closed but curious.

I knocked on his desk, hopefully for luck. "I think Jimmy's dealing in harder stuff, he called it a side job. He's given me four hundred for working on a friend's bike. You and I both know that's overpaying me."

"Then why take the money?" Teddy asked; he was being hostile. He didn't appreciate my line of questions. Teddy was a bear of a man, he was also grossly overprotective. "Kid was working with you for six damn months. He was by your side helping you out every time you needed him. This is the respect you show him for all that help? You flake out on him when he gets patched and now you accuse him of dealing dirty?"

"I took the money because I'm not a dumbass," I snapped at him. "But dealing out an extra four hundred bucks like it's nothing is suspicious, Ted. And I'm sorry I flaked, I don't have a good excuse for that." Though, I would call Madi a good excuse they probably wouldn't agree with me. "I'm trying to protect my interests in the club just as much as I'm trying to protect myself."

"If you want to protect your interests," Ted said as he stood, his fists clenched up at his sides, "then stay out of it. If you don't know anything and you're questioned by a cop, then you can't be implicated in anything we do. Keep your fucking ignorance." With that, he stalked out of the office.

It left me alone with Wilson and I tried not to let Teddy's temperament get to me. I prided myself on being a mellow, easy going guy considering all the shit I'd been through serving and then my discharge. It was hard to not let the distrust of a guy I called friend get to me. Wilson didn't let me stew in it.

"What have you got besides the money he gave you?" he questioned.

"He gave me the money to work on his friend's bike, a piece of shit he said he found in a rotted out shed. The guy stuck around while I did the work," I explained meeting his steely gaze. At least he was hearing me out. "Guy offered me a deal on Percocets when he noticed me having problems getting around. You know what Percocets are?"

"Oxycodone," he nodded, "I know what that is, I've taken them in my day. You think Jimmy is dealing in harder stuff with his friend?"

I looked down, studying the letters etched into my fingers. 'Don't give' was inked into the upper part of my fingers. It got questioned sometimes, but I took it as meaning 'don't give up' or 'don't give in.' Now I looked at them and I wasn't sure which I wanted it to mean.

"Yea." I looked back up at Wilson.

"You make accusations like that and you'll need to have something to back it up... beside just your word." He shifted in his seat and folded his tattooed arms over his chest. "Tillman vouched for the guy, he watched him work alongside you and bust ass doing grunt work that all the newbies do. Except for you. We gave you a lot of special treatment because of your situation." He spoke seriously like I was paying them a terrible insult by being suspicious.

"I'm not fucking special snowflake. I didn't ask for special treatment," I snapped, glaring at him now. "I've busted my ass just as much as Jimmy has. I've treated every bike you've put in front of me like it was better than my own Goddamn bike. I fucking helped with the plumbing when the bathrooms were backing up and I cleaned out the shit. Tell me that I haven't earned my patch, Wilson." I felt the heat of my anger burning up my neck. "Tell me that I've wasted the last four years of my life, motherfucker."

He raised his hands as if to ward me off, though he still looked the picture of calm. It was like my words hadn't affected him in the least.

"Not at all what I said," he said plainly. "What I'm saying is you see what the kid does around here, and that's all. When we do runs, things you aren't involved in, we see how the kid is. If you're going to accuse him of doing something that'll give us a bad name, I want you to supply me with something I can work with besides your word and your gut." He must've sensed that I was about to argue, that the fire of my anger still simmered at the surface. "I trust you, I know that you wouldn't come to me if you didn't think something was up. But for me to do anything about it, I would need something more than your word."

I stood, still angry, but I nodded. "I'll let it go then," I growled as I started to the door, I had to get out of here.

"Don't." He stopped me. "Don't let it go. Be vigilant. Keep your eyes and ears open. When you can give me something to back up your word, you come back to me with it. Don't mind Tillman. Let him be sore." I looked back at him. "But if your gut is telling you something is up, you follow your gut."

That was something. He was telling me he trusted me in a roundabout way. I guess that was something for my bruised ego.

13

I made a point to make myself scarce after that. Madi was still at work and I had a few hours before I could get any sort of comfort from her. I opted to go for a long overdue ride. The last time I had gotten on my bike was Wednesday, and then after suffering for a day or two, I spent the rest of the time with Madi. I didn't regret it. I'd been accused enough of being stupid in the last day that I wasn't going to actively be stupid by wishing I hadn't been with a beautiful girl. It was enough to have me watching the clock and waiting for the word that she was off work.

What do you do when your friends are pissed at you and your girl is working? I didn't have money I could play with, even with the couple of hundred bucks that Jimmy gave me. I felt like a sulking kid and I didn't want to let it affect how my attitude was when I met with Madi.

My option was simple. Go to the gym and work the anger out. This was how I kept myself mellow. I lifted weights and jogged until my muscles screamed and throbbed. I had to stop short, my ego still smarting. But by the time I hobbled out of the base's gym, I had a text from Madi letting me know she was off and headed home.

'I have the option of going home for a shower or coming over your house for a shower. If I come over to your house, will you take a shower with me?' I sent the text to her and tried to sop up the sweat that was sure to make me stink.

My phone pinged, indicating Madi's reply, 'I could be talked into a shower.'

'Good, I'm on my way. Get naked.'

I didn't wait for another response. I packed up my shit into my saddlebags and threw on my sweat-soaked shirt. I got on my bike, and I made my way to the girl that was sure to soothe my rattled nerves. I pulled my medicine bag and fresh clothes from my saddlebags as soon as I got to her house. It took me maybe thirty minutes and I had hoped she was naked when I knocked on the door. I knew better though and she let me in with her sweet smile. I felt better already. I left my figurative baggage at her door and let her lead me to her bathroom.

We undressed one another, the water was turned on, and I tugged her into the shower with the intent of doing something more than showering. I pressed her into the wall and silenced any sort of protests she might have had with a kiss. She didn't fight me. Instead, she held me close and touched me to the point that I forgot I needed an actual shower. She pulled her mouth from mine long enough to gasp out, "Need a condom."

I wanted to go in raw, to sink into her without anything between us, but I pulled away from her with a groan.

"Stay," I growled at her. I went into the bedroom, not caring that I was leaving a trail of water. The box of condoms was where we left it Sunday, and I was faced with the fact that there was just one left. Shit. I headed back to her, rolling it on without a care. "Remind me to get more." I gave her a look, seeing her soaking and hungry for me like I was her.

I got a nod, and before anything else could distract us, I pounced. She was back against the wall and I hefted her up easily, her legs around my hips. I was mindful enough to make sure she was wet, brushing my fingers against her clit.

"Now," she breathed against me. "I want you in me now."

That was all the encouragement I needed. I arched my hips and I was in her sweet hold again. My day did nothing for my need for her. If anything it made me need her more. I pressed her into the wall as I thrust into her. I laid my brow against hers and put every ounce of frustration from dealing with Teddy and Wilson into each thrust I made into her. She held onto me, gasping and clinging to me like I was a lifeline. I thrust into her until I felt her gasping, her nails digging into my back. When she started that vice-like hold, I kept going. I wasn't ready to quit yet. I pulled out and got out of the tight hold that her legs had on me.

"Stand up," I ordered.

As soon as her feet were on the floor, I turned her around and pressed her hands against the wall.

"Keep your hands on the wall," I commanded.

I didn't think this through and I realized that immediately when I went for reentry. She was significantly shorter than me. I was still dizzy with lust, so I managed to improvise on the fly. I contributed that bit of genius to the Army. Unable to crouch to the point I needed to, I just hefted her up so that I could slide back into her. She moaned and I shifted her closer to the wall, angling my body away from her as I began to thrust into her again. It must've been a good angle because the noise she made was even louder. It was something for my ego, so I hefted up one of her legs and kept going. Her head fell back onto my shoulder.

"Don't stop, don't stop," she began again.

It became a chant for her that was broken only by hitched breaths and moans. I realized she was cresting on another orgasm and it made me feel damn good. I let go of everything and began to just enjoy the feel of her against me, the hold she had on me, and every little noise she made. My legs began to shake as the effort to just keep throwing myself up into her was becoming too much.

"I'm gonna cum," I managed in her ear. "If you're close let's finished together."

I got a nod and I watched one of her hands disappear from the wall and drift down to where we were connected. I watched as she circled her clit with her fingers. I groaned and buried my face against her neck. It was so fucking hot.

"I love you," I gritted out because once that shit was out, I wasn't going to be able to keep from saying it. It didn't seem to affect her anymore though. If anything she squeezed me harder and I was erupting into her. She cried out and quaked in my arms, seeming to follow me into bliss.

I had her pressed against the wall and I was soon aware of my own trembling. I gently let go of her leg and carefully pulled out of her cunt so I could settle her on her feet. I didn't pull away though, I stayed pressed against her back.

"That was…" she panted, not trying to escape me, "intense."

"I might've been angry before," I admitted.

She looked over her shoulder at me, her brows drawn up. "I don't think I've ever seen you angry."

"I don't get angry often," I assured her. "The water's gone cold we might as well wash up and get out." I shakily stepped away, keeping a hand on her and a hand on the wall to make sure neither of us fell. "You good?"

She nodded. "I'll help you wash up then we can get out."

She slipped out between the wall and me, plucking up the bottle of soap I had stashed over the weekend. She went about lathering up my back, from my shoulders down to my ass without pausing a beat at the scars that went from my hip down.

"Do you want to talk about what made you angry?"

I shook my head, my eyes fluttering closed at the feel of her hands on me. She pressed into my back, her hands came around to go over my chest and down my stomach. She pulled the condom off of me and stroked me clean, I was over sensitized at first and winced even though she handled me gently. I kept my hands on the wall as she stroked me then went down to cup my balls in her soapy hands.

"You're going to get me hard again and I'll have to push you back up against the wall to fuck you again."

"You just used the last condom." She moved so that the soap was washed away.

"Then I guess," I straightened and turned around to face her, "I'll have to go to the store." I cupped her face, stroking her cheek. "I can't seem to get enough of you."

She didn't turn from me, but she reached behind her to turn off the cold stream of water. She gave me a smile that made me ache.

"I can't say that's a reason for me to complain." She pulled away from me then, her face still flushed. "Let's get dried off, we need to talk."

Uh, oh.

I followed her out of the shower and made quick work of drying her off than myself. A knot started to form in my stomach and I opted to tie the towel around my waist when I followed her out of the bedroom. I sat on her bed and watched as she dressed. Then I watched her pull out clothing for me; a pair of boxers, a shirt, and jeans.

"They got left here over the weekend," she said as she handed them to me. "I washed them and figured I'd give them back to you." She sat beside me. "Offer you a little room to bring things over if you wanted to stay the night."

"If I wanted to stay?"

She didn't look at me, but she shrugged.

"You say all these sweet things to me." She brushed her hands through her wet hair. "You tell me you love me and you want me for keeps. That you won't break my heart." she looked at me then. "Maybe we could see what it's like to make things more serious. I liked waking up with you beside me."

It seemed that at least one thing could go right for me today. "Not moving in, but staying over more frequently?"

"You said it was too soon for moving in the last time I mentioned it."

I shrugged, unable to keep from grinning. "Did you already clear out a drawer for me or something?"

She rolled her eyes and finally looked at me. "I didn't clear out a whole drawer but I could if you would need it." She sounded nervous. "If you would want it?"

I hadn't got the L word out of her yet, but from talks like this, I imagined she was close to admitting it. I nudged her with my shoulder.

"Do I get a key, too?"

"Are you making fun of me?"

"No, no." I stood and started getting dressed, slipping on my jeans and pulling on a shirt. "But this conversation just made things worse. You're probably going to need to just resign yourself to spending the rest of the day in bed."

"Oh!" She tried to give me an aloof look that I saw right through. "Well, I guess that's just something I can live with if you're planning on making it worth my while."

I took a second to pull my combat boots on before I turned back to her to give her a good long look. "If I get a key, baby, you can look forward to walking funny in the morning," I said to her as I walked out of her room and headed out the door.

14

I hadn't moved in with Madi, but after she gave me a key to her house, I spent more time at her house than my own apartment. I would get a text here and there from her asking me to stay the night with her. It was maybe a night a week that I'd stay at my own place. I didn't ask her to stay the night at my place, though if she were to ask I wouldn't protest it. Maybe it had something to do with the fact that her place was definitely better than mine.

That said, things at the bar were pretty much the same though it was clear that I had rubbed Teddy raw. I made sure to give him space and paid attention to the shit I had to get done. And I kept an eye on Jimmy, though he hadn't made himself scarce. If anything he hung out around me more, flaunting his patched cut and bringing his friend, Anthony, around more frequently. They also brought me another bike to work on, this one in better shape than the first. They overpaid me for the work again, but who was I to complain?

On the second day of work on the damn thing I heard them talking lowly. "Greg's got an order cooking. How quickly do you think you can move it?"

Anthony hadn't made an effort to lower his voice in the least. I think, maybe, he thought he could win me over in the same fashion that he did Jimmy. Maybe he was thinking that I'd be another jackass to sell his shit. I made an effort to keep my face blank as I worked on putting the carburetor back into place.

Jimmy hissed low at his friend, "Just let me know when and I'll be there."

I watched them out of the corner of my eye, the work I was doing was so ingrained I could probably do it in my sleep. I saw Anthony nod towards me and the other shook his head. I had to wonder if Teddy had said something to him. It was probable, depending on how much I had pissed him off. But, if that were the case, I probably wouldn't be sitting here working on this bike and getting overpaid. I was determined to keep an ear on them though.

I finished up sooner than I expected and I looked back at them. They still looked like were talking shit.

"You want to come crank it for me?" I called out.

"You can't crank it yourself?" Jimmy asked with a glare.

That patch had turned him into less like the guy eager to help and more into an ass trying to swing his dick around.

"Well, motherfucker, sitting on my ass on tore up asphalt for the last two hours has kinda got me stuck down here." I was definitely going to need a hand up to do anything. I'd have to walk off the aches before I could get on my bike to ride home.

"Quit being a dick," Anthony said, giving Jimmy a sour look. He came over and helped me to my feet. "You never dick over the guy that's working on your bike. There's not a lot separating you from the road, so you definitely don't want to piss off the guy that knows just what bolts to loosen that will make your bike fall to pieces while you're riding it."

Sound advice. I hobbled around to get feeling to get back into my good foot.

"Sid's got morals," I heard Jimmy say like it was an insult, like morals were an STD or some shit. "He wouldn't do anything like that." He came to stand beside me as I was shaking out my left leg. "Would ya?"

"Sorry, dude," I shrugged my shoulders, "not going to implicate myself in anything."

It wasn't something I would do, but I wasn't going to deny it though. I felt suspicious looks from the younger man but I didn't meet his gaze. Right now I didn't really care what he thought. Jimmy shook his head at me and sat on the bike. With little effort, he kicked it to life and the engine growled lowly just as it was supposed to. Anthony whistled and offered me a hand, I took it and was pulled into another one-armed hug.

"You are like a magician, my friend," he said before he stepped away. "I didn't think that would be something that you could manage."

"Unless it's completely rusted out it's not hard to get something like this purring again. I'm sure you're smart enough to see a complete loss when you see one." I shrugged not know what more to say.

"If you did bodywork we could probably make more money," Jimmy said as he shut off the bike. "I hear there's a lot of money that can be made in custom bikes."

"I think you watch too much TV." I grimaced at him. "Those shows only cater to rich assholes. I seriously doubt there'd be anyone around here that would be able to afford a custom bike, much less want one."

"I don't know," Anthony said beside me. "I might."

"I don't do bodywork." I looked between the two of them. "I spent about eight to nine years working on engines and being trained on the changes that they made to the various trucks they commissioned. Bodywork wasn't something I was involved with."

"I can respect that." Anthony nodded. "I have a friend that dabbles in it, kind of a learning as he goes thing. So far he says it's a pain in the ass. Remember the first bike you worked on for me? He's trying to get that one cleaned up to the point where we could sell it. So far, it's giving him hell."

I nodded as I listened. "What's the issue?"

"The frame is good as it's not rusted like we first thought. We're just trying to avoid replacing all the exhaust.

It had a unique look to it that I liked." He shrugged then sighed. "But it looks like I may not be getting my way with that."

"So it's more along the lines that you're giving him hell about having to replace the exhaust." Jimmy chuckled. "And not the bike."

"Whatever." The other man waved it off, and they started to load up the bike. "I'll see you Wednesday night. Sid, it was a pleasure doing business with you."

I gave him a wave and went to hobble inside. My phone buzzed at me and I didn't resist looking at it. I grinned when I saw the request from my girl about coming over for the night. That was enough to distract me. Then Jimmy bumped into me.

"Thanks for helping Tony with his bikes," he started, nudging me as he stepped around me. "Dude seems to like you. If you want to do more business with him, let me know. He's got a couple of different ventures that he's into."

"I appreciate it." Though my gut told me that the other ventures were less than legal. "I think I'll just stick to shit that I do around here though. Keep my ass out of trouble, ya know?"

"If you get tired of just getting by day to day, let me know," he said lightly as he made his way to the bar. "You know, in case you ever want to give your girl anything nice."

I frowned; that was low. I'd have to ignore it though. I decided I wasn't going to start anything and I would just keep my cool. I went towards the office, giving the door a knock until I heard Wilson growl out a 'come in.'

"I'm about to git." I just stuck my head in. Predictably, Teddy was in there, too. Both of them usually took up the office, if that weren't obvious by now. "Do you need anything from me before you go?"

"Nah, kid," Wilson answered, sounding pleasant which was unlike him.

"You been taking off and blowing us off quite a bit," Teddy piped up before I could duck out.

I stood in the doorway for a second with my phone in hand before I decided how to answer to that.

"Well, I didn't have a regular broad for the last four years." I could only offer him a shrug because it should be obvious. "The chick that served you seemed interested and has kept me distracted. Is that going to be a problem?"

"Cindy says he has it hard for her, too." Seeing Wilson speak up for me was something. He was a man that didn't seem to be overly cozy with anyone. This was the first time I ever saw him stand up for anyone. "Give him a break. Just because Doris left you doesn't mean the kid can't find an old lady."

"Cindy's a rat? Remind me not to tell her anything else private," I grumbled.

"Why do you think I keep her around, kid?" Wilson grinned at me and I got a mental picture of the two I would rather not have. I pinched the bridge of my nose in an attempt to clear the image of the two fucking from my head.

"Do you need me for anything?" I asked again because I didn't want to leave and have something come up while I was gone. I didn't want my ear to be chewed on tomorrow.

Teddy grumbled but shook his head. It was apparent that he was holding a grudge.

"Fuck off for a bit, Tillman," Wilson said before looking at me and waving me to enter the room.

Teddy rolled his eyes and stood, edging past me with a growl. I closed the door behind him and looked back at Wilson curiously. "Did you need something?"

"You got anything on Jimmy since we last talked?"

I hesitated but remained standing in the office. I wasn't sure where to go with it. I was pretty sure Wilson was a man to trust. He held everyone with a critical look in his eyes and didn't take bullshit. I grimaced and nodded.

"His friend brought me another bike. He seems to think whatever they're running I'll get in on, too." I shrugged and rubbed the back of my neck. "There was something about a guy named Greg cooking something and Jimmy moving it, they're going to meet Wednesday night."

I watched as Wilson scratched at his beard, seeming to think on what I told him.

"Can you follow him?" The older man finally asked.

"I'd be pretty obvious on my bike." I didn't like where this was going.

"Your old lady got a car? Take that." He sniffed as if it were no big deal. "If Jimmy is getting into meth, like this suggests, then he isn't the right fit for us, and he needs to be taken care of."

"I can't mess up my chances with this girl," I argued. "It's still too new to be asking favors like that. I don't want to fuck things up."

He raised a hand as if he sensed I could keep going. He waved around my worries and went back to petting the beast of a beard that hung from his chin.

"I'll get you a car, I'll put the key in your saddle bag and you'll find it parked across the street. If you're willing to back up your word with proof, I'll handle it from there. And I'll handle Tillman, too."

I stared at him for a moment, trying to decide whether or not I wanted to threaten my chances with Madi. She was important to me. But if Jimmy got too careless with what he was doing it could threaten everything I held dear. I nodded.

"I'll keep tabs on him."

15

"I'm taking Wednesday off," Madi said to me as we got ready for bed. It gave me pause and I looked at her. I waited for her to supply me for a reason and I stood there with my jeans hanging around my ass, just looking at her. "I have a doctor's appointment."

I opened my mouth to speak, but her explanation seemed to hit me like a ton of bricks.

"Isn't it soon for you to suspect you're knocked up? We've been careful." I gave her a hard look at, trying figure out if she looked pregnant. She flushed at me, and I realized that I probably didn't ask that in the nicest way. She was still beautiful, but I couldn't tell if there was this mystical glow that pregnant chicks supposedly got.

"Not what I have a doctor's appointment for," she huffed, but didn't look too angry. "Does the idea of having a kid scare you that much?"

"I haven't put a ring on it, yet. So... yeah." I looked away from her as I pulled my jeans the rest of the way off and sat on her bed. "I want to do right by you and knocking you up before I made this... well... permanent. Kinda knocked the wind out of me." I sat in just my boxers, taking her in as she pulled a t-shirt over her head. Seeing a bike across her breasts made me realize she was wearing one of my shirts. "Would you let me make it permanent? Or would you throw me out on my ass if I knocked you up?"

She shrugged and came to sit next to me. "I don't know. Kids weren't something I was thinking about right now." She looked nervous and glanced away.

A shot of fear went through me and I wrapped an arm around her shoulders. Now it wasn't a matter of her being knocked up, but that something could be wrong.

"So, what's wrong?" I watched her for any sign or tick that there was something going on, that I had a reason to be afraid.

"I thought maybe, I could save us a buck," she shrugged. "I'm going to get on birth control." I blinked, trying to process what she was saying. "I thought, maybe, we could enjoy each other without something being between us. It... it'll take a week or so to be sure that it's working. But maybe we could take a special night and just..." She turned and leaned against me, her lips brushing against my cheek. "Be together?"

I groaned knowing where she was getting at. "I really need to put a ring on this girl." I flopped back, letting the stress that had suddenly coiled up in my gut go. "I can't let her go." I tugged her down to me. "You thought you were stuck with me before, baby." I tilted her chin up so I could kiss her. "You're definitely not going to get rid of me now."

She kissed me before I could manage. "Maybe I don't want to be rid of you."

She broke away from me for a beat, her eyes were dilated and the little bit of green I could see was so dark. If I ever doubted this girl wanted me before, I knew better now.

16

When Wednesday rolled around I was kept busy; Wilson had fucked up his shit on purpose it felt like, and I was piecing it out like I hadn't done so damn near a month ago. Either he didn't give a shit about it, or he was just fucking with me. Sometimes I couldn't tell. Jimmy helped me at some point before Teddy put him on some sort of errand. I couldn't piece together if he knew what Wilson was having me do. I found the key Wilson had promised in my saddle bag when I took a break from my work for lunch.

I had already taken the extra measure to let Madi know I wouldn't be staying with her for the night. When she inquired as to why I hesitated to answer. I didn't want to tell her the truth. Especially after I made an effort to make her believe that the Brotherhood, the guys I rode with, were all good guys; that we didn't do anything illegal. I opted to let her know that I had a job that was going to take me longer than I thought to finish.

It wasn't far from the truth, I told myself as I gave Wilson's bike a hard look. This fucker usually made sure I spent the majority of my day working on his damn bike.

I managed to piece it back together before Jimmy headed out. When I heard him cry out to someone inside that he had shit to do, I booked it to the sedan that Wilson had parked in the lot across the street. Fucker had me running and I did not manage to look good running with the limp I had going. When I got in, I made sure that shit had gas. Fortunately, Wilson's sense of humor wasn't that vicious. I waited until I saw Jimmy slide out of the lot on his bike before I cranked up.

I had to be cool with the length that I followed him. There was this awful temptation to go without lights and I did before he turned onto a well-lit road. I made sure my lights were on before I pulled back behind him. He rode out into the country, seeming without noticing me behind him. I was surprised to see him take his bike down a dirt road. I avoided dirt roads simply because I didn't want to get shit all over my bike. His always looked clean, so I gathered he either cleaned it after these visits, or he didn't usually take his bike. I doubt it was that latter. He was kind of like me in the sense that his bike was the only vehicle he needed. It only made a difference when it rained. For him, because he was fortunate enough to serve and get out without injury. It just meant he would get wet if he had to get out. For me, I was stuck indoors and usually in a cloud of drugs and pain.

I went straight to not draw attention to myself, and I cut the headlights then did a U-turn. I swung around and went up the dirt road. Jimmy already had a good distance on me, but as far as I could tell the dirt road didn't have any houses running alongside it. I didn't know if it was fortunate or unfortunate that the moon was bright enough for me to see a trailer in a wooded lot. I rolled the car to a stop. It was evident people were in the trailer, but I didn't see anyone outside. I opened the door and didn't bother closing it. I tried to stay low and use the darkness to hide me as much as I could.

Only, I didn't get very far into the yard. There was a roar of engines coming from behind me. I thought for a second I was fucked, and Jimmy's friends had caught me. When I heard the sirens, I wished that had been the case. Two police cruisers tore around the car I had used to get here and thrashed the yard as they pulled closer to the trailer. Another set of cruisers pulled up behind my car and I knew I was trapped. I didn't even bother, I put my hands on my head and waited for further instruction as I watched the cops swarm the trailer. They ran past me and at first, I thought I'd gone unnoticed, but a sharp voice soon barked for me to get on the ground.

I sighed. "Alright, but I have to warn you I'm a wounded vet and will require assistance getting up."

"I said get on the ground!" was barked back at me and, with an effort, I refrained from rolling my eyes.

Getting on the ground wasn't easy. It was late and it had been a long day, so the knee of my left leg decides not to cooperate. I end up flopping forward into the grass and groaning when things got aggravated. I put my hands back on my head and just waited.

I heard the doors to the trailer thrown open followed immediately by yelling and cussing. I looked up to see if Jimmy was forced out, but so far I had only seen the lit doorway. A shot was fired, though I could only hope the kid wasn't that stupid. There were sounds of a struggle, but soon it ended, and I saw Jimmy being walked out in cuffs. As well as Anthony and another guy that I can only assume was Greg. Jimmy's eyes connected with mine and he bared his teeth at me.

"Did you fucking rat on us, Redding? Did you call the fucking cops?"

"Nope," I hollered from the ground. "Otherwise I wouldn't be laying my ass on the ground getting arrested, too, Dipshit."

My side was nudged, and I didn't bother to look to see who did it. I just watched as they struggled to get the other three men into the back of their vehicles. A knee was pressed into my back, and I grunted. The pain suddenly intensified, and I gritted my teeth as the guy on me brought my hands down to be cuffed.

"Cooperating, no need to get rough," I winced.

"Okay, bud, time to get up," the officer that cuffed me said without commenting on my complaint. His hands came up under my arms, and with little effort on his part,

I was tugged to my feet. On my part, however, the move was excruciating.

"I'm going to need my pills," I gritted out between clenched teeth.

"That what you were coming up here for, junkie?" He actually chuckled at me. "You're going to have to wait to get your next fix there, man."

"Wounded vet," I said again as I was shoved towards a car. My limp became more pronounced as my left leg got stiffer. "You keep this rough treatment, man, and you're gonna have me an incoherent mess."

I got the Miranda act read to me as they forced me into the car, my left knee bent under the force of the hand on my shoulder. I couldn't help but cry out in pain as the act of bending shot through my nerves. Yea, I was looking at a night of being an incoherent mess of pain. I had one fleeting thought before the throbbing started to take over.

Did I get fucked over out here?

17

When the cops did a search on me, they found my earlier warnings were true and then managed to fish out my identification. I had started sweating in the cop car, and at first, the guy thought I was overdosing or something. I managed to hike up my jeans leg enough to give him a glimpse of the mangled, burnt skin. Normally, I didn't try to play the sympathy card, but I was fucking hurting and I needed some relief. If they let me cook in a holding cell the pain would only escalate and soon I would be hugging the metal shitter and throwing up all that I'd eaten that day. It's not a pretty sight when the pain gets too much. I hoped they didn't let it get to the level where it was too much.

"Make your call to someone that can get your medication," the officer that was checking me in commanded. "Get your shit here because if you puke up my holding cell, you will be the one cleaning it up."

I grunted in acknowledgment and picked up the phone that was offered to me. I punched in Teddy's number because his was the first that came to mind. I didn't remember anyone else's, and he'd picked me up on more than one occasion. It was after midnight, and I honestly didn't care if I woke him up. The phone rang and rang and, fortunately on the fifth ring, he finally answered.

"What?" was croaked into my ear.

"I was arrested, I don't know Wilson's number. I need my drugs." I knew I didn't need to say who it was. Granted, he probably didn't expect a call from me.

"Why were you arrested?" He sounded confused, and his voice was muffled for a second. I heard movement suggesting he was getting out of bed, "The fuck did you do?"

"Followed Jimmy," I growled at him. "Bring me my fucking pills and see how long I've got to sit in a cell for this shit."

I didn't give him the chance to question me longer, I hung up the phone and let my temper stew. I limped to a cell, getting one to myself with a guard to watch me. I figured that they thought I might keel over, and after all the flak that law enforcement has gotten recently, having a vet die in holding is bad press they'd like to avoid. Maybe they assumed I was decorated.

The holding cell was just a cement box with bars closing off one end. There was a cement bench with a thin pad on it. I guessed that was as good as I was going to get for a bed. I hobbled to it and sat with my back to the wall, and my left leg stretched out. I didn't get any relief since I was stuck waiting for Teddy. I tried to focus on breathing, I tried to massage my leg through my jeans, I tried every single pain management technique the cute physical therapist tried to teach me as a means to get through it without pills. I lost grasp on time when I did this and it felt like hours had gone by when it really was only a few minutes before a cop came in with my medicine bag.

He and my guard went through it carefully, studying the contents of each bottle to make sure each was prescribed by a doctor. All of my medications were VA approved and I struggled to stand as I watched them. I needed my nerve pill and my anti-inflammatory pronto. I doubted they'd be nice enough to give me a Valium to get me through the night. I stumbled and nearly fell, which under any other circumstances would have been embarrassing. Now, it would have been inconvenient in the fact that I wouldn't have been able to get back up on my own. I got to the bars, and I waited anxiously for them to offer me something. I found myself leaning against the bars because the longer I was left standing, the shakier my stance got.

"Which do you need right now?" The officer that had my bag eyed me. I guess it was apparent how bad off I was.

"Nerve pill and anti-inflammatory." I rubbed at my face, trying to get some clarity. "If you're cool the Valium will take the edge off."

"There are so many pills in here, man," they complained but took the time to feed me the ones I asked for. "Why the hell are you on so many? You're only thirty it's kind of messed up to be on this many."

I swallowed the pills dry, choking on the nerve pill. I didn't care. It meant I would get relief soon. I had a paper cup filled with water offered to me, and I downed it in a single gulp.

"Caravan found an IED," I explained. "Assholes like to bury bombs in roads that we frequented."

"You got all your limbs though," the officer holding my bag argued. "I've seen some guys come home less an arm and a leg after that."

"My truck was on the far side of the blast," I patted my left leg, "far enough away to offer me some protection, but I still got burnt up when the engine of the truck went. The doctor wanted to take this leg, cut me off below the knee. But it wouldn't have helped the sciatic nerve pain I would have to live with, so I declined the option to be a pirate." I pressed my forehead against the cold bar. "How long am I stuck here?"

"For the night at least," the guard said. "You have to wait until eight tomorrow morning for the judge to get in and set bail."

"Fuck me," I sighed and turned to go back what would be my bunk.

"Can I ask with all the good shit you got here, why you would be going to a trailer for more drugs?"

If I was smart, I would've said I wasn't talking without a lawyer. But, I got to where I was, so obviously

I'm wasn't that smart. "Wasn't there for drugs, had no clue what was going on in the trailer." I sat down heavily. "I was following my friend there to see what kind of dumb shit he got into."

"So, you're telling us you just got dragged into the dumb shit, too?" my guard asked.

"Yep." I settled in, going back to the drug-free pain management methods that didn't work. "Would be glad to offer to do a drug test, you'll see everything I'm on is in the bag."

"I saw the dash cam footage," the officer with my bag said to the guard. "Dude just stood there and waited when he saw the cars come flying in. Didn't try to resist or run. That shit hardly happens with people whether they're innocent or guilty."

"Aside from the fact that it's dumb as shit to run," I offer up. "I can't run for shit."

"Man, you can barely walk right now." He held up the bag. "We're going to go through these and get your next round ready. Try to sleep."

Easier said than done.

18

Sleep was fleeting, and when the Valium kicked in, I stopped caring about both the pain and my situation, so I managed a light doze. I got maybe four hours. The problem with pain is it fucks up my grasp of time. The guards eventually got me up and gave me my pills. I declined another Valium, even though I already had the aches. I wanted to be sober for what was going on.

I waited for my turn in the arraignment line, for a chance to see the judge and to find out what exactly I was being charged with and what my bail would be. I realized I'd probably end up stuck here and the realization made my stomach turn.

I could've called my parents, they lived a few hours away and probably would have booked it here to make my bail and see to it that I got a decent defense lawyer. But that would come at a consequence. My mother had been dying for me to come back home, wanting to take care of me like I'm an invalid. I've had my freedom since I went to boot camp… though I use the word free loosely because really I just took it from my parents and sold it to the government. I didn't really become free until after I was discharged.

But here I was in cuffs with ankle bracelets to match. A guard stood next to me to make sure I wouldn't do anything stupid or to keep me upright, I couldn't tell.

"I've never been arrested before," I said to him. "How long does this shit usually take?"

"Judge is usually quick, they try to process people as quick as they can so those that can afford to make bail, do. Do you have an attorney?" He eyed me curiously, seeing my patched cut and combat boots.

"I spent about nine years in the Army," I said with a shrug. "Fuck no, I don't have money."

He snorted then tried to choke back his amusement.

"Don't do illegal stuff. Plus, cut the cussing. Judge Fredericks is not a fan of it and will probably add to your bail because of it. He considers it a sign of bad character."

"Fantastic," I sighed. "Telling me not to cuss is like tell me to stop breathing." I got another laugh from him and, had the situation been different, he was probably likable. "You gotta motorcycle?"

"My wife would kill me." He paused and eyed my cut. "Your club push drugs?"

I knew what he was fishing for and I shrugged my shoulders. "The club I'm in caters to vets and retirees. People that ride in the Veteran's parades and shit like that. We don't deal with drugs. You should see the bag I gotta carry around full of prescribed drugs; almost as big as a woman's purse." I shrugged, the chains that connected my wrists to my ankles shaking. "The Boneyard Brotherhood is kind of like a support group with motorcycles."

He nodded, and we shifted as the line moved along. He offered me decent banter that seemed to make the wait move along at a quicker pace. I was good as long as I didn't have to dwell on what was going to happen after this. Because nothing good ever came from being arrested, even if you were innocent.

When I stood in front of the judge, I listened to the charges with growing dread. I knew Jimmy and his friends were either in front of me or behind me in the line for this. I hadn't bothered to look for any of them, I was more worried about myself than them.

"Felony manufacturing charges with the intent to sell," one lawyer said simply. She was a blonde woman with hair that touched her shoulders and had a dark pantsuit on.

"How do you plea?" The judge asked without looking up at me.

"Not guilty," was my answer, because of course, I was not guilty.

The judge looked up at me with a critical eye. "Says here you are a serviceman? A wounded veteran?"

"Yes sir," I met his gaze without any sort of hesitation. I knew I was innocent. "Served two tours in Iraq and the last one ended my career with the Army."

"I would like to know the outcome of the trial that comes after this." He taped the gavel. "Bail set for two thousand."

I grimaced and was moved along the line. My bail was set, but I was sure that I would probably be stuck because I sure as shit didn't have the money. I was taken back to the cell that I had spent the night in, and I expected to sit there until my trial date.

I tried to not think about what would happen from there. But it's was near lunch, and I could only imagine that with her work, Madison had found out by now. I rubbed at my face as I tried to figure out her reaction to it. It was hard to guess. I wouldn't know until I talked to her and the not knowing just tore me up. I spent the remainder of my day letting the worry eat at me. At six a guard came to get me.

"Somebody made bail," he said simply and walked me to collect my shit. The progress was slow going even though the only 'weapon' I had on me was a small pocket knife.

I walked out of the holding part of the jail. To my surprise I found Teddy and Wilson waiting on me, both dressed in suits and looking less dirty biker and more like prepared adults. I stood just outside the door that had released me from jail, just standing there staring at them.

"Who the fuck are you guys?" I chirped.

"Funny," Wilson growled at me as he adjusted his suit coat, it looked a little tight on him and didn't really make him look like a businessman. He looked like an adult that might have his shit together... might being the keyword. "C'mon let's get out of here so we can talk business."

"I don't want to ride bitch," I complained, and I heard chuckles from behind me. I imagined that Jimmy probably didn't have the same experience I did. I eyed them both as I followed them out of the jailhouse. "Where's Jimmy?"

"Jimmy bailed himself out," Teddy said without venom. "If he knows what's good for him, and he's smart, he'll stay away from the bar for a while."

They led me to a car which surprised the shit out of me. It was a late model town car.

"Whose car is this?" I realized both of them were older, but I didn't expect them to drive around grandpa cars.

"You call me old, you bastard," Wilson snarled at me, "and I will bust your ass so hard you won't know what hit you!"

He closed the distance like he was going to do just that. I raised my hands up like I was under arrest again and that seemed to placate him enough. We loaded up, and I waited until they were both settled before I let my anger get the best of me.

"So, which one of you assholes decided to set me up?"

"Neither of us," Teddy said as he glanced over a shoulder at me. "It doesn't benefit the club at all to set up one of its members."

"Really? Because the night I go to follow Jimmy out to do his meth pick up, a shit ton of cops that roll in." I didn't keep the sarcasm from my tone. "This is after you,"

I gestured towards Wilson, "arrange it so I can follow him. Tell me how that doesn't sound fucked up?"

"I'll give that to ya," Wilson said lightly. "I set up a cheap car without a plate so in the event something went down it wouldn't be traced back to the club more than it already would be, considering two members were caught in a meth lab," he grumbled and looked to Teddy. "The kid is going to have to be out, and we will be shutting down all illegal activity for the next six months. Shit'll be tight." Teddy nodded, listening intently. "We'll have to pool our funds to make sure this jackass doesn't get pinned with something he wasn't involved in."

"Done," Teddy answered without hesitation. "I'll get on the phone with the attorneys in town and see if I can't find one that'll cut us a deal."

I listened to them talk, leaning back against the seat and letting the weariness and lack of sleep catch up with me. My phone was clutched in my hand. I assumed the police must have turned it off after they searched through it for any sort of pertinent information for the case they were going to build against me. I was sure my terrible attempts at sexting were looked through with amusement.

I knew that the slim black device held nothing but bad news for me. Did Madi know? Her reaction was something I wasn't sure I wanted to see. She didn't strike me as the type to get violently angry. She seemed meek at most points, and while I didn't want to take advantage of that, I was worried how she would take this. I knew she would probably feel betrayed after the way I talked up the club and swore there was nothing illegal that we did. I swallowed and decided the best route was to take it like a man. I ripped the fucking band-aid off and turned my phone on. After a slow bootup, I was notified that I had six text messages and a voicemail. I started with the text messages, figuring they would be the easiest to handle.

A simple one from Wilson was received at eleven pm: 'Check-in'. He probably got worried when I didn't show up back at the bar.

The rest were from Madi.

At ten-thirty pm, I got a sweet 'Good night. I'll miss waking up to you.' with a little heart symbol. My chest started to hurt.

At seven thirty, she sent me a 'Good morning,' with a smiley face included.

It was just after nine am that I got the next one, 'Getting kind of worried. Usually, you're blowing up my phone. Are you okay?'

I was attached to this girl, I didn't try to harass her, but I wanted her to know how much she was on my mind. I didn't leave her hanging.

'You were arrested? Please, tell me this is a joke,' was the last one from her. I could feel my heart sliding into my stomach.

The last text message that I read was from Jimmy. 'I'm gonna fuck you up when I see you.' I snorted and shook my head.

"Jimmy's going to be after me now."

"While I don't doubt you could take the kid," Wilson said without looking back at me. "I will make sure I put him in his place."

"Let me do it," Teddy started to argue. "I can handle Jimmy."

"No," I heard Wilson snap in response. "If you would have listened to Redding in the first place we wouldn't be out the money it's going to cost to get his ass out of the fire," he growled in a low tone. "Instead of listening to his gut and taking his word with some consideration, you pitched a fit like a bitch. You should consider yourself lucky I'm not making you scrub toilets with your toothbrush."

They went back and forth like that for a little while, I rolled my eyes. I tuned them out and decided to hazard the voice mail. I held my phone to my ear and waited for the final verdict.

"I thought you said that you didn't do anything illegal, Sid." Her voice sounded choked. I closed my eyes and brought a hand to my forehead so that the other two men in the car wouldn't see any of the emotions I was feeling. "How could this happen?" It was clear she was talking to herself. "I want my key back." The message ended, she sounded broke, and I felt it.

I'm such an ass.

I dropped my phone in my lap and tried my best not to let the emotions choke me. My throat burned and I clenched my eyes closed, trying not to cry. I definitely didn't want to cry in front of these bastards. I feel the car turn and we were parked in the lot that was in front of the bar. Teddy and Wilson got out and I stayed in the back of the grandpa car, trying to pull my shit together.

Teddy lingered by the car, I noticed when I got out and tried to wipe my cheeks so that it didn't look like I was wiping away tears. He gave me a look like he had an idea what I had been doing.

"Let it blow over, show her you're innocent," he said softly. "She'll forgive you."

I followed him across the street, and we started towards the bar door when I saw my bike. There was a bag on the seat, and I knew without a doubt that she had packed up all my things. I was going to be cut out because of this. It tore me up and I didn't bother going to the bar. I picked up the bag and shoved it into the closest saddlebag. I picked up my helmet and sat on my bike. I was tired, and now all I wanted to do is fall in my bed to dwell on the end of that one slice of heaven I had managed to taste.

"You're gonna go?" Teddy called out to me.

I gave him a nod, put my helmet on and kicked my bike to life. I needed to get out of there, I didn't want to be emotional in front of anyone.

19

I spent the majority of the day in bed, only getting up when I needed to and taking my pills when it was time. As soon as what was necessary was done, I flopped back on my bed. The mattress was too firm and was nowhere near as comfortable as Madi's bed. Her sweet scent wasn't anywhere and I couldn't even smell her on me. The only thing I could smell from my sheets was my own stink and the lingering smell of motor oil. The smell of oil never seemed to leave me.

In a short amount of time, I had managed to get things going good for me. I had a girl that took a good portion of my attention. Our exchanges were easy, and after she had got used to me, she opened up like a flower. The shyness that had stilted her when I first spoke to her went away after our lunch and I enjoyed every little conversation we had. Her voice was soft and it warmed me just to hear her speak.

There was no one here but me. There was no conversation going on in the tiny apartment I called home. It was just me in there, laid out across my bed dwelling on the noise in my own head. I didn't have the soft feel of her body against me or the light snore of hers to occupy the room.

I was alone. Really, I hadn't been alone since Teddy picked me up from the bar. I made the effort to keep myself surrounded with people to keep myself distracted. The idea of people now seemed stifling. I didn't want to go to the bar. I didn't want, or care, to find out what happened to Jimmy. I didn't want to face Teddy's concern. Would he apologize for the shit he gave me when I first mentioned my concerns to them? Did I even care?

Part of the problem with being alone is that there was nothing to distract me. There was nothing to keep me out of my head. I had stopped taking the anti-depressants and anti-anxiety pills; medications that had been prescribed with the worry of PTSD. It had been a long time since I actually thought about what happened in Iraq. I spent the majority of my time in the desert working on any vehicle that was put in front of me and I had duty like everyone else. My job had been easy and I very rarely had to fire my gun for anything other than practice. I had been tapped to drive in the caravan that would carry supplies out from the base to the village that was closest. The IED didn't even blow under the truck I was driving. It had hit the truck that had been rolling ahead of mine, killing three of the soldiers within and crippling the others that were lucky enough to survive. The guy that rode shotgun with me had the same kind of burns that I had, though the distance from the blast made them a little less severe.

There were groups and they offered support in the form of a bunch of men and women that had been wounded. We all struggled to figure out a way to get back into life, to let go of what had been taken away from us and go back into normal society. Sometimes it was just a bunch of men and women staring each other, doped up on the drugs that we took that were supposed to help us forget what had put us there. It was supposed to help us cope, but more often than not some decided they would have been better off biting it. So they would take the matter into their own hands, for relief from the pain.

It had been what I was considering when I first met Teddy. Chewing on the nine millimeter that I kept in the closet and pulling the trigger to get relief from the pain and the noise in my head. When it was quiet in my room and I wasn't numbed by alcohol, I could still hear the noise of the IED exploding and the ripping of metal.

I thought that I was over this. I thought that the roar of my bike's engine had drowned out the sound of the explosion. The pain was something I was told I'd live with the rest of my life. But, the noise and the smell of death was something that had been replaced by wind whipping in my ears and the smell of the road. And all of that had been replaced in a short amount of time by the sound and feel of a girl.

I hadn't been kidding when I told her I loved her, even though I had jumped the gun. I knew she felt something for me. If it wasn't love, it was close to coming to it. With that gone, how was I supposed to cope now?

20

I found a dusty bottle of whiskey in one of the cabinets in the kitchen. I hadn't drank seriously since I joined the Brotherhood, save a beer here and there. Now, I forged through my bare apartment for any alcohol that had survived the last few years of being in the Brotherhood. I needed to be numb.

I had no idea how many days it had been since I was out, how long it had been since Wilson and Teddy had bailed me out. I didn't know if it was night or day. I didn't care. A knock on my door didn't get my attention either, as I had turned off my phone and hadn't bothered to check in. I wasn't going anywhere, so they didn't have to worry about me skipping bail. Needless to say, I didn't answer the door. Unfortunately, I forgot about the spare key I had given Teddy. I watched my front door open and the big man came in; Wilson was right behind him. I hadn't even heard their bikes even though I had been just dwelling on the quiet of my room.

"You dead in there?" Wilson called when he saw me looking.

"Not yet," I grumbled and rolled onto my back. "Give me a couple of days and I might be." I groaned and pulled a pillow over my head. "Fuck off!" I really didn't want to see either of them.

"That's not going to happen," Wilson growled as he came into my apartment and thundered into my bedroom without asking permission. "We're not going to let you do stupid shit because some bitch dumped you for being stupid."

I was up and in his face before my brain even caught up with what he said.

"Madi," I growled, "is not a bitch." I felt like I was ready to throw down for this, the alcohol was really messing with my frame of thought. "Say it again, old man," I hissed at him. "Let's see how that goes."

His face went red and I could see him sizing me up, trying to figure out whether or not he could take me.

"Sit your ass down," he growled back at me. "Ain't no sense in trying to try to uphold her honor if she's not here to see it or if she's not with you."

I waited to see if he was going to give me a reason to punch him. I wasn't happy to see either of them.

"It's been a few days," Teddy said as he came to join Wilson in my bedroom. "I understand your reason to be down and out, but not this far gone." He looked at me even though I was still glaring at Wilson. "You're back on the edge and because of what? A woman?"

I sat heavily on my bed. All I wanted was to be alone.

"I'm not contemplating the flavor of my gun," I assured him. I cupped my face in my hands, trying to cover the view of any sort of emotion that I had been feeling that was bleeding through. I wanted to be alone and numb. Them coming in and bringing up Madi wasn't going to help my issues. "I just need time to be alone," I grumbled.

"We're not going to give you any more time," Wilson snapped. "You've had two days. That's enough."

I growled at him and pulled my hands away from my face, "When was the last time you had a serious relationship, old man? Are you married? You don't know me, you don't have the right to tell me to get over a woman I was in a relationship with that got broke off because of something I was doing for you. You have some serious balls to come in here and tell me to get over it like you know how I feel. I've made enough sacrifices for you assholes. Don't come lookin' for me to make more."

"Not what we're here for," Wilson snipped, moving to lean against one of the bare walls of my bedroom.

"We're here to help build your case for you." Teddy folded his thick arms over his gut and glared at me. "We all know you're innocent and why you were there. Making a case shouldn't be too hard. Have you contacted the VA to learn about the state of your benefits?"

I shrugged because as of right then I didn't care. I had already gotten paid for the month, why should I fret over something that wouldn't affect me until the first?

"Let's say," he sat next to me as he spoke, "we prove your innocence. If that girl is as tore up about this as you are, maybe she'll see that she was wrong to drop you like the sack of shit you are."

I grimaced at him. "Do you think Doris would give you a second chance?"

He looked away, the pain of his failed marriage apparent on his face. Teddy knew how I felt. I didn't doubt this man cared for the woman that left him. And I'm sure that me pointing out his failed relationship was enough to give him insight on how I felt.

"You won't know if you just let her go," Wilson grumbled, making it obvious that he wasn't keen on being a part of this conversation. "If you just let her make up her mind and not put up any sort of fight, then you're not worth the shit on her shoes. Women like to be fought for. If you just let her go because you make one screw up, then you're not a real man."

"Words of wisdom from the old man?" I asked because the usual banter between Wilson and I was me calling him old. He would get so angry that he would start looking like a bulldog. "Did you live this shit, too?"

"No," he snapped. "I'm not a dumbass like the two of you." He turned and walked out of my bedroom, going to scope out of the rest of my apartment. "We got you an attorney that's going to take your case pro bono, and he even promised to ensure you keep your disability. You meet him on Monday. Sober up."

I cupped my face in my hands again, pressing my fingers into my eyes. I wasn't hung over, but there was a good chance that I might have been drunk. Though I didn't feel like it.

"What day is it?" I asked, unable to ascertain the information myself.

"Saturday," Teddy said after a length. "You make this effort to save what you got with this girl," he looked at me hard, "and I'll make the effort to save what I had with Doris."

"Why did she want a divorce?" I asked because I had only met his wife once or twice over the last four years that I had known the guy. He always seemed like a caring guy, though I thought this because he picked me up off of a barstool when I was at rock bottom.

"Because," he stood up and started out of the room, "I can't take care of shit at home, and I would rather be on my bike than on my wife." I watched him walk out of my bedroom and he left my apartment with both Wilson and I watching.

He knew what his issues were with his wife. I could see, after blurrily thinking back to what I could remember of the last four years that I'd known him, what he was getting at. He was at the club day in and day out. I knew because I had been, too, up until about a month ago. After which I had been spending as much time as I could with Madi.

"You coming, Sid?" Wilson stood at my door, glaring me as if he were daring me to tell him no.

I sighed. "What are we doing?"

"Getting your shit together and your ass out of trouble," he snorted like it should have been the most obvious thing. "C'mon, we've got a guy waiting for you at the bar that'll help us out."

"I'm probably drunk," I inform him as I stood back up.

"You also need to put pants on." He sneered at me. "Don't come outside with your dick out or I'm not responsible for Teddy kicking your ass. There's a good chance I might help him."

21

While I wasn't as bad off as I assumed, I was still stuck riding bitch on the back of Teddy's bike. Their excuse was that they didn't want to put anything else bad on my record, like a DUI.

"We gotta keep you squeaky clean to get out of these charges. So sit your ass on the back of the bike and shut the fuck up," Wilson barked at me.

"Fine." I sounded like a petulant brat, but there was nothing like having to wrap your knees around a hairy man. Especially one you thought screwed you over.

On the bright side, if the ride managed to wake up ole' boy downstairs, it would be my dick against Teddy's ass and not the other way around. I had to pick which one made me more uncomfortable. I wasn't entirely sure the amount of alcohol I had consumed in the last few days, so there was a good chance that ole' boy would be too numbed up to care about the rumble and vibrations of the ride. I didn't get a punch after the ride, so I figured he behaved himself.

"Guy was in the service, too," Wilson explained as he went to the bar door. "He's not a criminal attorney by trade, but he's willing to throw us a bone when we need it. So listen up and be smart about this."

I nodded, deciding the best way to do this was to sit and listen. A 'do as you're told' kind of deal. When we entered, I saw a man in his late forties sitting at a table with a plate of wings in front of him. He wore a suit and looked clean cut. He didn't really seem the type to hang out at the bar for fun. Wilson and Teddy went straight for him. When they filled up the table I grabbed a chair from another and sat down. This should be interesting.

"Warren Michaels," Wilson gestured to me. "Sid Redding. I got this kid in trouble now I need your help getting out of it."

Warren offered me a hand and we shook. He nodded as he eyed the wings in front of him.

"Nice to meet you," he said to me. "I told you before that I don't normally do criminal law. But I did some research on the case and evidence. The video they have of you stopping and standing with your hands on your head is pretty telling. You cooperated the entire time. They also have a record of your medications as well as the piss test you did. All of which matched." He paused and took a sip of the tea that was also on the table. "A criminal, like the ones that were in the trailer, usually resist and attempt run. That's something that's gotten you the right amount of attention. First thing I need to ask, why were you there?"

"One of the guys that was arrested is in the club," I started.

"Was," Wilson cut in. "We're working on filling his ass right on out of here. We don't have a need for assholes like that bringing cops around here."

I shrugged and kept going as if I hadn't be interrupted, "I had a hunch that the guy was into something without authorization from either of these two." I hooked a thumb towards Wilson and Teddy. "Wilson told me to keep an eye on him and see if I could get evidence that he was. But, it seems like the cops were following too." I glanced at Wilson and Teddy now, I wasn't going to hide what I had been thinking the last few days in my haze. "Or they were tipped off."

"You can blow that out your ass if you think it was anyone from here," Wilson growled. He looked back at Warren, his face scrunched up in distaste about the idea I had planted. I hoped I pissed him off; if they had just taken my word for it the first time I mentioned it, we wouldn't be in this situation. "How fucked is he?"

"Assuming that they manage to drag him through the dirt and find something on him that I couldn't," he picked up a chicken wing and eyed it like he was trying to decide if it was good or not, "I say we have a fifty-fifty chance. If you had the medal of honor, it would be even easier. But one of the drawbacks," he looked to Wilson, "is all illegal activity that is done by the club has to stop now."

Wilson nodded. "We're going quiet to our suppliers, they know what's up. All the people we dealt to also know to find their stuff elsewhere."

I blinked slowly and looked at the three men sitting at the table with me. "He knows?"

"My wife," Warren answered for Wilson and Teddy, "has stage three breast cancer. Right now pot is pretty much the only thing that is keeping her eating." He shrugged and looked helpless, his brows drawn together and every wrinkle of his face stood out starkly. "I can't lose her. I got to try to do every little thing possible to help her beat it." He cleared his throat, seeming to realize he was exposing his emotion. "I was introduced to Wilson through a mutual friend that met him through one of the parades that the Brotherhood participates in. He's been getting me a supply for Karen for the last six months. I can't... You have to stop." He looked hard at Wilson. "Paint this a picture so that you look like the VFW or a Legion outpost."

"It's stopped," Teddy said seriously in response. "I will get you the name of a man that can fill our spot while we go clean."

Warren nodded. "I will get that before I leave. I do have a suggestion for what you can do in the meantime to generate funds." He took a bite of the wing he had in hand, realizing it was better than he anticipated. He took the time to finish it before he wiped his hands clean and went into a briefcase. "Set up a legit business, something you and your men can offer that won't draw the hard eye of the law."

"You got suggestions? Everybody here served at one point or another," Teddy asked curiously. "A lot of us have struggled to find work in the real world. Opening a legit business isn't going to make things easier."

Warren took the time to eat another wing as he considered the options. Humming lightly as he enjoyed the flavor of the chicken. Cindy was a helluva cook and those wings were delicious.

"I'd say you could turn this into a restaurant and sell these for a good buck," he said around a mouth full.

"No," Wilson shook his head. "I don't want to put any kind of stress or distraction on Cindy. Besides she is paid under the table."

I was also sure that he had something on the side with her. Though, I wasn't sure if Wilson was married or not.

"There are other ways," he mumbled as he started to work on another wing.

"Why not open a shop?" I asked. It startled the shit out of me; came out of nowhere. They all looked at me, eyebrow raised in question. "Car shop... bike shop. A garage." I shrugged as I struggled to explain. "Not a chop shop, but you bring your bike to me at least twice a month for a tune-up. There are a couple of other guys that know their ways around an engine. Open up a garage. Make that a legit business."

"First smart thing I've ever heard you say," Wilson spoke lowly as if it were true. I gave him a one-fingered salute. "That could actually be feasibly done."

Warren nodded and started wiping his hands clean.

"I could actually look into some places that would work for that. It'll help you draw revenue for this while you have to stay under the radar." He looked from Teddy to Wilson. "It'll take work and some money to get it started."

"We've got enough to outright buy a place," Teddy said lightly. "But it'll be in our best interest to probably take out a loan. I think we can get to work on that part if you can give us some leads for a place without distracting from Redding's case."

"I've got a friend that I'll get to help you out with a legitimate business plan," he assured him. "I don't intend to get distracted from this."

I listened to them chat for at least an hour before I had to get up and stretch. Pins and needles assaulted my left leg and I needed to walk it off. I wasn't being questioned anymore, it was just more them setting up a game plan. My head was still fuzzy and I wasn't really into the idea of talking mechanics about how they would get me out of the charges that were against m, or how they would make the club look like just a bunch of vets hanging out.

I made my way to the bar and knocked on it. I would've called out to Cindy like I usually did, but I wasn't into it.

"I'm cleaning up, pretty boy." She peered out of the kitchen at me. "If you want food you are shit out of luck."

I shook my head, and the world tilted a little. "Do I have a stash back there? I left my important stuff at home."

She went back into the kitchen and set down whatever it had been she was cleaning. She came back out with a sandwich bag that had some pills in it. I couldn't even tell if they were my usuals or not. She set the bag on the bar top and went about fixing me a healthy cup of water. "I don't know how long I've had them back there, so if they're out of date, they're probably not going to help you much."

I picked up the bag and eyed the pills hard. The big nerve pill was in there and I was sure there were some painkillers in there, too. I shrugged and fished out what I needed before I tossed the small handful back. I chugged the water and sighed, the relief wasn't instant, but the water helped set the world straight for me.

"You heard from Madison lately?" Cindy asked as she leaned down next to the baggie I left on the counter.

I shook my head. "Not since I was arrested."

She leaned onto the bar and studied me. "Have you tried to get a hold of her?"

I shook my head again. I had pretty much chalked up the failure that it was. I was still trying to swallow it; though, for the most part, I was choking on it. This was a fuck up you don't really come back from. There were a select few women that would tolerate something like this and with her job, I should've known that Madi wouldn't be the type to put up with it. It hurt and it'd probably hurt me for a while. I didn't bother trying to tell any of this to Cindy. She was smart enough to read it on my face.

"So," she leaned close so when she spoke it was just between the two of us, "you tell this girl that you love her." She paused for a beat as her watery blue eyes sized me up. "Then when shit hits the fan you let her go? Did you not want this to be serious or were you just in it for the sex?"

"That was the most sex I've had in the last four years," I told her with a grunt. "I haven't worked right since I got discharged." I sighed and propped my head up with a hand on my forehead. I eyed the pills in the bag so I wouldn't have to just look at her. "I love her, but she can't take heat at work. She's got a house note to take care of and car trouble that's probably going to crop up again." I shook my head. "I can't cause trouble for her."

"Normally," she started slowly as she seemed to consider what to say to me, "I would say if someone can't hack the hard stuff they aren't worth the trouble. You're making excuses for her not to hack it. If you love her, like you say you do, then you need to show her the truth. Show her you're innocent and if she still doesn't want you then," she shrugged. "you're not at a loss, she is."

"I can't bring her trouble," I started to argue.

"It's not trouble," she knocked on the bar, "it's love. And if you're thinking how you feel about her is going to bring trouble then maybe you don't love her like you think. You just like the fact that your dick gets hard around her and she's happy to help you out." She turned to head back towards the kitchen. "Sex doesn't equal love, pretty boy. It's a crying ass shame that you can get to be this old and not realize that."

I grimaced and found myself wondering if she was right. I shifted to sit on a bar stool and spent the rest of the night reconsidering how I felt about Madi. It felt like love. My chest ached like I had taken a bullet. It hurt to breathe. I had the need to see her but I didn't have the will to accept the rejection I would probably face. I poured my heart out to her once. I'd be up shit creek if I did it again and she still told me to fuck off. There was only one real option I had, aside from cutting my losses and letting her go. I had to see if there was still a chance.

"Go in the morning," I heard Cindy call from the kitchen. "Don't be a jackass and wake her up in the middle of the night."

22

After it had gotten late enough for them, Teddy carted me back to my apartment.

"You're not going to be stupid, are you?"

He went the extra mile of walking me to my door. Like he thought I was going to go in and go back to hitting the bottle. All my bottles were empty and I was broke for the rest of the month. No more hooch for me. But I waved away his concern and went inside to crash on my couch. Exhaustion hit me and I crashed hard, not caring about the time or how uncomfortable my couch would make me.

I don't know how many hours of sleep I managed, but as soon as the light hit my eyes, I groaned out in protest. Goddamn me for having the bright idea of drinking my sorrows away. I sat up and stretched out slowly. My back ached, my hips ached, and my left leg was all pins and needles. Plus my head throbbed and it felt like I had a mouth full of cotton. I struggled to my feet and stumbled into the kitchenette for water. I also needed to start my pill regiment for the day. I went about my morning in a blur, not quite sure what exactly I wanted to do with myself. I didn't have an epiphany about my situation until I was soaping up in the shower. I had been running on autopilot and my general idea was to lurk at the bar like I used to. It didn't require thought, and someone might throw me a bone with something to work on.

"If I want something," I said aloud as I began to rinse, "I should fight for it."

Cindy was right. So was Wilson. I got out of the shower and decided the best thing to do was see if there wasn't something to hash out with Madi. I dressed, opting for a pair of jeans and a simple black shirt. I put my stash into my saddlebag and hopped onto my ride. Time to face the music.

I felt lucky when I saw her car in her driveway followed by immediate dread. The last Sunday she and I spent together it was mostly us just laying in bed, alternating between snoozing and sex. What I wouldn't give to just be curled up next to her in bed. I sat in front of her house as I tried to steel myself. There was a very good chance she would turn me away, and there was nothing like having a woman tear up your heart right in front of you. I still had her key unless she went the extra mile to change her locks. I couldn't be a dick though. I couldn't just go barging into her house.

That decided, I got off my bike and followed the little path to her front porch. My bike had already announced me. If she was home, she would have heard me pull into the quiet little neighborhood. I pulled out my keys and fished through the ring until I came across hers. I held up my key on the ring, looking at it hard like it had the answers as to how to fix this; like it could tell me what to say.

I knocked, keeping her key in hand. If she demanded it, I would have to give it up. I knew this and I couldn't argue. It was hers after all. But maybe, I could get her to see reason. But the door remained shut. I looked at the little hole covered in glass, and I wondered if she was glaring at me through it. Did she hate me? I knocked again, straining my ears to see if I would be able to hear anything.

"I know you're home," I said to her door. "I just..." I paused feeling like a jackass. "I just want to explain what happened. I've not lied to you so far, and there's no reason for me to start now. Give me the chance to tell you what went down before you decide to cut me out."

I got silence, and I knocked again, a little harder. "Madi, please." I pressed my brow to her door. "Please, c'mon."

There was no answer and it was decided. I started to work her key off the ring.

"For what it's worth," I could hear my voice crack with emotion, "I'm innocent. Something along the lines of being in the wrong place at the wrong time. I followed Jimmy out there because I had a feeling he was getting into some bad shit." Once I had her key wrestled off my ring I held it up to her peephole in the event she was looking out it. "I have court in a couple of weeks, come find out for sure if I'm innocent if you want."

I stood there, waiting to see if she would open the door; if she would say anything. I got nothing.

"I meant it, you know," I said against her door, being quiet enough so I didn't have to worry about her neighbors hearing me embarrass myself to her. "I love you. I get why you're doing this, but I think you should at least hear me out." I tapped the key against her door. "I promised not to break your heart if you promised not to break mine."

Still nothing.

"Fuck," I sighed and turned.

I tried, right? There's an A for effort, right?

I sat down heavily on her front step and tried not to let her lack of an answer get to me. I kept her key in my hand as I tried to figure out where to go from here.

"I guess this is it, huh?" I said to the key like it would give me an answer. "No chance to argue my case, no chance to beg for forgiveness. I get fucked over not once, but twice; both in a serious way."

I turned so I could put the key on the doormat, grimacing as I felt the tightness in my chest start to burn its way up my throat.

"I wouldn't have done this to you, just so you know," I said to her door again. "I would have given you the chance to explain yourself because I love you. Because you do enough for me that I would want to forgive you and not lose you... I guess it's not the same for you."

I forced myself up and trudged my way to my bike. I had to get out of there before I broke. I had to be strong. There's nothing like putting up a front for how broke up you are. I got on my bike without a real thought of where to go, letting the grumbled growl of my bike soothe me.

23

I decided to go with the original plan for the day. I got to the bar and started work on the first bike I saw. It was Wilson's, of course. I didn't bother asking, just pulled out a small toolbox and started giving it a tune up I was sure it needed. It was near lunch when I started to shine up the chrome on his bike and someone noticed I was there.

"The fuck are you doing?" Teddy asked.

"I need a distraction," I said not bothering to look up as I ran a polishing cloth over a chrome exhaust pipe.

"And you're cleaning up Wilson's bike instead of your own?"

I gave him a look and nodded to my own bike. It sat in my usual spot, shining without a spot on it. If he cranked it, he would have heard an unfettered growl to its engine.

"Touche," he chuckled. "What's going on? Why do you need a distraction?"

"I went to see Madi," I said lowly, giving a glance to the rest of the lot. We were out there alone. "Didn't go well."

"Ah." He looked away, not looking like he had anything to offer.

"You want me to do your bike next?" I asked as I went back to work.

This bike would probably look good for the first time in years, Wilson was the kind of man that road shit hard and didn't bother to take care of it outside of what was necessary. When Teddy patched me in it had become my job to do the maintenance on his bike. I was okay with it.

"Sure," he hovered over my shoulder, watching me work. "D'ya need to talk about it?"

I stopped, looking at his distorted reflection in the chrome. Was this his way of reaching out? Teddy was a stubborn man, he would beat his head against the wall before he'd admit he was wrong. I glanced over my shoulder at him and I saw remorse looking back at me.

"Talk about what?"

"Your woman issues," he snorted at me as he found a cigarette in a pocket of his cut and pulled it out. "I can't claim to know much about them. I've only been married to Doris for fifteen years before she decided to call it quits." He paused to light the cigarette and inhaled sharply, "Fucking Wilson was right though. If you don't make an effort to fight for them and let them think you're not interested anymore, they don't have a reason to stick around."

I looked away from him and started to pack up my shit. "I tried to fight. She didn't even make an effort to listen. I get the feeling I was barking up the wrong tree. She's not in it for the hard stuff and I got a lot of hard shit going on. Not just with this shit." I threw down the cloth, and I struggled to my feet. "If you would have just fucking listened to me... opened your Goddamn eyes... maybe I wouldn't be in this situation." I looked at him hard. "If you had fucking listened to me, neither of us would have gone to jail. I might still have the girl of my fucking dreams instead of being here shining fucking bikes because I don't want think about what I just fucking lost."

"Blame me," he shot back at me. "I deserve it because you're right. Jimmy is Doris's nephew. What right do I have to believe family over you?" His tone had gone sarcastic and he waved his hands as he spoke. "What has Jimmy done for me besides bust his ass?"

"And I haven't busted my ass for you?" I snapped back. "I don't have any stake in this club and all that it does? Do I ever make shit up for giggles?" I took a step towards him, baring my teeth as I spoke. "Have I ever done you wrong?"

He seemed to relent then and shook his head. "No." After a length, he looked me in the eye and sighed. "I'm sorry, kid. I fucked up your chances with that girl and you can hold that grudge against me for as long you want. Blame me for it all." He threw out his arms. "Hell if I left you alone where do you think you'd be now?"

Six feet under, but I didn't tell him that. I know over the last few days I had considered it. I backed down and rubbed my hand against the back of my neck.

"What do I do now?" I sighed.

Teddy relaxed, I guess he could see me for what I was: a directionless asshole. He shrugged.

"Do what you need to keep your head on straight. Worry about what you have control over and do what it takes to keep yourself out of trouble, like Michaels said."

"What about the idea of the shop?" I asked out of curiosity, I remembered pitching the idea, but I didn't know what was said after that.

"We're going to move forward with it." He fished his keys from his front pocket. "We got a building that's ready and can support that kind of business. I'm going to go through the guys that need work, legal work, and see what their mechanical training has been." He tossed the keys to his bike at me. I caught them easily enough and it distracted me from the anger that still throbbed in me at his man. "I mentioned you should manage it and do what you can for pay. Help get you out of that shit hole you call an apartment."

"Don't judge my shit hole," I grumbled and started picking up my tools.

"Smudge his bike back up," Teddy chuckled. "Fucker won't recognize it looking so clean."

I started to make my way to Teddy's bike without bothering anymore with Wilson's.

"Then point it out to him if he starts to think his got stolen," I called back. "Let me know when you get shit started for the shop, and I'll do what I can."

Any distraction would be a good distraction was the way that I saw it.

I spent the next couple of weeks doing it like that. I had a while before the trial and I was determined to keep busy. I decided to not let any of it dwell in my head. It was work and if the Army taught me anything, it was better to have work on your hands than to be idle. So I worked on everyone's bikes regardless as to whether or not I was asked to. I did work around the bar, replacing some rotted out wood and even climbing my ass up onto the roof to replace shingles. After I climbed down the ladder, I saw Wilson waiting on me with a scowl.

"The fuck did I do now?"

"You got a suit?" he asked, eyeing me as if I were something he had to look at and found distasteful.

"Why would I?" I picked up the ladder to take it around to the little shed that sat behind the bar. "Do I look like a man that'd own a suit?"

"You'll need it for trial. You can't show up in a courtroom in jeans and a t-shirt covered in grease." He followed me as I walked. "You've got a lot going for you in your corner and it's in our best interest that you don't look like some sort of punk kid."

I snorted in amusement as I sat the ladder in the shed. "Ain't I a punk kid?"

"Exactly," he grunted at me as he leaned back against the wall. "We've got to paint the picture of you being an upstanding citizen that was just at the wrong place at the wrong time. At least part of that will be true." He chuckled to himself. "Give Cindy your size, I think she can probably find a decent one."

I groaned, but I couldn't argue. We went back into the bar to find the attorney waiting for us.

"This why you came to hunt me up?" I asked curiously.

"We do need to start preparing you for trial," Warren spoke up from the table he was parked at. He already had a plate of wings and a pint of beer on the table. "Give you an idea as to what you should expect and how you'll be expected to behave."

I went to his table to join him. "I don't get to just sit there and look pretty?"

Warren chuckled in amusement, and I heard Wilson growl out, "Fucking kid."

"No." He shook his head. "While that's the majority of what you will be doing, sitting there and listening, it's in your best interest to pay attention and try to do your best to keep from looking bored. If you fall asleep, that can pretty much be a nail in the coffin for you." He looked down at the meal before him and seemed to be considering his words. "You might be asked questions and it'll be smart that you refrain from using profanity." He looked at me. "Will the majority of your tattoos be covered by a suit?"

I didn't have any on my neck, and the only ones that I couldn't cover were on my hands and fingers. I held up the back of my hands. "Unless I wore gloves, though I think that would be kind of lame."

Warren nodded in agreement. "You can keep your hands off the table and it'll be a little less telling. It'll be pretty easy to clean you up and have you presentable looking next week."

"I'm fine with cleaning up as long as I don't end up in jail for something I didn't do," I told him stiffly. It's not that I didn't think I could hack jail, it's just that I didn't want to hack jail, especially when all I was doing was keeping an eye on someone. If I had to wear a monkey suit to keep my freedom, I'd do it.

24

Of course, the trial was something that would creep up on me while I tried to ignore the stress and depression which were curling their fingers around my throat. I was so bound and determined to work my way through it that I had to spend the entire day before the actual trial scrubbing all the oil off my hands and working to make sure that I got the grease from under my fingernails. Cindy got me a suit that was only a little tight in the shoulders. When I tried it on for her, she whistled low and eyed me in a way I wasn't used to from her. Despite the fact that she enjoyed calling me 'pretty boy.'

"If I were twenty years younger, boy," she started as she helped adjust the jacket for me. "I would make it so that you walked funny."

"Jokes on you," I shrugged, not liking the feel of the wool on me. I felt trapped and cramped in it. "I already walk funny."

I was given a white linen button down and a simple tie to polish off the yuppie look. Honestly, I would have preferred my dress uniform to this crap. I still had it in the back of my closet. I wore the shined up shoes from it so there was at least one thing that kept me from feeling too out of place. Really, I felt more at home in my uniform than I did in this monkey suit. It didn't help anything. All the preparing just made it harder for me to sleep.

So, I kept my work lighter and I spent the majority of the time chewing my pills and having my TENS unit taped to me. The night before, I had Wilson eyeing me with something that looked like concern.

"Are you going to need that tomorrow?"

I shook my head. "Even if I do hurt, I'll just suffer through it. It'll keep me from falling asleep."

"You got something you can take for that?"

"I got something that'll make me look stoned," I leaned over in my seated position and propped my elbows up on my knees. "Pretty sure we don't want me looking high."

He nodded and moved as if he were going to leave me alone now. But he paused, standing just a short distance away from me.

"I'm sorry," he said after a length. "This would have been a whole lot easier if we just took your word for it."

I nodded, not sure what to say because truthfully all this would have been avoided if they had trusted me.

It all came back to that. There was a lack of trust from Wilson and Teddy. There was a lack of trust from Madi. If they had just followed my hunch and questioned Jimmy they might have realized that I was telling the truth. Then I wouldn't have been arrested and Madi wouldn't have been forced to choose something. Our relationship was still new, so it was asking too much to expect her to stick with me. I realized that and I didn't find myself angry with her, though maybe I should be. It didn't seem fair that she didn't even give me the chance to explain or defend myself. But, I guess it wasn't fair to ask her to take on this stress.

"Yep," was all I could say.

A hand fell on my shoulder, and I felt it squeeze lightly. "I'll do what I can to make it right."

25

The trial was both boring and frustrating. There was a list of my crimes, and the prosecution painted a picture of a wounded warrior turned junkie due to the number of medications I was on, a few of which were narcotics. The lady had a very viable picture of me seeking a better high by abusing methamphetamines. I'd never really been big into drugs. The only times I ever got drunk were more for a means to just numb my thoughts. Though, considering the fact that my medicine bag looked more like a pharmacy, and the list of prescriptions I had, I could see where she was getting at.

Fortunately, Warren was quick to point out just what the drug screening reported. I only took the medications that I needed to function. Taking all the others didn't seem to have the desired effects and that was something I was willing to testify on. However, I didn't get to testify at all. If anything all I got to do was sit and look pretty as my fate was argued between my attorney and a pretty lady that seemed all too eager to put me in jail.

This apparently was what the legal system passed for nowadays.

Fortunately for me, there was far too much evidence provided that proved that I was innocent. When the judge struck the gavel down on his bench, it was ruled exactly what I was. I was innocent; just a fool for being in the wrong place and at the wrong time. I got a steely-eyed look from the man in the black robes and a stern, "Don't let me see you in my courtroom again."

I saluted and gave a convinced, "Yes sir." I didn't need to be told twice.

After that, it was our queue to leave. I turned, waiting as Warren packed up his things, and spotted a familiar brunette leaving the courtroom. Granted, brown hair was pretty common. I hadn't heard from Madi since I was arrested, much less seen her. But at that brief sight I had to see if it was her for sure; if I could catch up. I shifted around Warren and breezed past Wilson and Teddy, trying to get out of the courtroom in a rush.

The hallway was empty of the brunette I had spotted, so I followed the small crowd and filed out onto the steps of the Greek-inspired building. I didn't see Madi. I looked at the cars that lined the street and didn't spy her little sedan either.

Maybe it wasn't her.

The idea made my chest hurt. She didn't show up, and she didn't care.

"Why'd you run out?" Teddy snapped as he panted, probably having run to catch up with me. "That's a shit way to show your appreciation for getting you out of bogus charges."

"I thought…" I ran my hand through my hair then grimaced. It was stiff from an effort made to make me look less like a dirty biker and more like an average Joe. "I thought I saw someone," I explained before turning back to him. "I guess I was wrong."

He shrugged at me and I could tell he knew what I was talking about.

"You could always go try to track her down if you think it was her." I shook my head. I was tired and the stress from the last few weeks had finally built up. Maybe I imagined her. "If you don't want to," he came closer and put a hand on my shoulder, "we can go back to the bar and have a celebratory drink. We still have a lot to do and plans to make for the shop."

I nodded because I didn't really have a choice; we all had come in Wilson's grandpa car. Riding a motorcycle in might have garnered us the wrong kind of attention. Plus, it would have wrinkled the monkey suit I wore. It had been dry cleaned, and while I had no idea who it originally belonged to, I was going to make sure I had it cleaned again before I returned it.

"I'm ready to get out of here," I admitted. "So the sooner we can leave the better."

"I'll go get Wilson and Michaels so we can hit the bricks," Teddy offered and left me out there.

Had she been here? Or was it just my heart playing tricks on me?

26

I stumbled into my apartment, not drunk, but dead tired from the entire events of the trial and the celebration afterward. I drug my fingers through my hair, trying to loosen up the stiffness from the product I used to give myself a respectable look. When I looked at myself in the mirror that morning while wearing the borrowed suit and having my hair slicked back, I was afraid of what I saw. I could have been a businessman or a yuppie, instead of a man that worked with my hands and lived to get dirty.

"Thank God for dodged bullets," I muttered to myself as I tugged off the jacket and started to loosen the tie.

There was a knock at my door holding me up from getting comfortable. I growled out a curse and went to answer it. I wasn't keen on celebrating my proven innocent, so if it was Teddy or Wilson, I was prepared to tell them to fuck off. I jerked the door open, the curse on the tip of my tongue. I held it though, dumbfound by who I saw on the other side of my door. It was like at the courthouse when I thought I saw her... I was struck.

Madi stood at the door, her hair loose around her shoulders and she wore a light blouse to go with a charcoal pencil skirt. She had taken on a relaxed look, like when she and I first started dating, it looked like she decided to keep it.

"Hi, Sid." She gave me a nervous smile.

I shook off the shock of seeing her and tried to mirror her smile, but it didn't feel right.

"Hey, Madison." I thought I'd say her full name because it had been a little while since I last spoke to her. "Did you..." I paused, trying to keep from losing my cool. I rubbed the back of my neck as I eyed her, I could feel my dick starting to betray me by just reacting to her appearance. "Did you need something?"

"I was hoping I could talk to you." She fidgeted with hands in front of her, looking down and away from me. "May I come in?"

"Sure." I stepped away from the door and opened it further for her. I watched her enter and it was like I hadn't gotten her smell out of my nose or the feel of her out of my memory. It took all my damn restraint to not hug her to me. But she decided when she cut contact with me that she didn't want me anymore. "What did you want to talk about?"

I watched her take a breath then she looked at me, her green eyes huge behind her glasses and determined.

"I need to tell you that I'm sorry." That caught me off guard. "You were right."

These were two things a man never expects to hear from a woman in one night.

"If I had bothered to analyze the time we had together before actually going to your trial," Madi paused then continued, "I would have known without a doubt that you were innocent." I swallowed hard, she had been there. "I know you aren't a terrible person." Her voice lowered, and I watched her shift from one foot to another as she seemed to collect what she wanted to say.

"Thanks." I kept my voice low, not wanting to give her any sort of distraction. "I appreciate it."

"I'm a terrible girlfriend," she blurted out suddenly, her face flushing. "I didn't support you or believe you when you were telling the truth. I assumed the worse and found out that it wasn't true."

She used present tense on that, I noted. "You say that like you are still my girlfriend."

Her gaze dropped and she paled. It wasn't until then that I realized how harsh I sounded when I said that.

"I wouldn't deserve to be," she said lowly. "You never asked anything from me. You never made demands for anything other than a little bit of my time. You gave me so much and then the one time you run into a little trouble... I abandoned you."

I didn't make an effort to reassure her. Since my arrest I had felt like shit and I can only imagine what having her around to lean on would have done to alleviate the stress that I felt. I know I wouldn't have been as depressed and it probably would have been easier to get distracted with her. I missed her and seeing her here made me realize just how much. My chest hurt and my throat felt tight as I processed what she said. She wanted forgiveness.

"You still want me?" I managed to ask.

"I never stopped wanting you." She took a step closer to me. There were only a short few feet between us now. "I just didn't know how to handle what was happening and the only thing I could think to do was put distance between us. It seemed like a good idea, and it seemed like the safest thing to do. I couldn't get hurt, and I didn't have to worry about getting into trouble, too." She released a breath and reached forward, her hand skimming over the button down I wore. "Is there any way I can make it up to you?"

"I don't want you in any kind of trouble." My voice felt thick and it felt like it was hard to talk with as tight as my throat had gotten. "I'd never do anything that would get you in trouble. You know that, right?"

"I do now." She edged closer to me and there was barely a breath between us.

I could put my arms around her and feel the relief of having her close to me, but I waited. She'd made me go through all of this I was going to make her feel some grief like I had.

"I should have known that in the beginning." Her voice sounded small and she looked at where her hand rested on my shirt. "You are the first person to tell me that they loved me and mean it. I knew when I heard you say it the first time that you meant it. Every time you would say it there was a ring of truth to it. I just..." she paused and looked up at me. "I just didn't realize how I felt until I had to go without you."

I wanted to touch her so bad. But I didn't want to distract her from what she was saying.

"How do you feel about me?" I asked, locking my eyes with hers.

"I love you." It was breathed out like a whisper, but it hit me right in the gut.

If I had any reservations about doing anything with Madi they were gone after hearing her say those three little words. I didn't even give her the chance to say anything else. I closed the little distance between us that was left. I bent down and I caught her mouth with my own. I cupped the back of her head and tilted her back so that when her lips parted, I could thoroughly taste her. I might have groaned when I dipped my tongue into her mouth. I missed the sweetness of her flavor just about as much as I missed the rest of her. It made me want to taste every inch of her.

Her hands clenched at the button down that I wore and I felt her give it a slight tug. That was enough for me. I gave the tie a final pull, and I ripped away from her to pull it over my head. I didn't even bother with the buttons of the shirt when I tugged it out of my pants and over my head to follow the tie. I felt like I had been at arms length with everyone, and now that I had the one person that I wanted right here with me, I was going to do all that I could to feel every inch of her. I worked my way backward in the direction of my room. I needed her. She followed me like maybe she needed me in the same way.

Now that I had my shirt out of the way, her hands trailed up along the length of my chest, skirting around my pecs causing the muscles to twitch. Her touching embroiled me more and I reached out to start unbuttoning her blouse. As soon as I had it open, I pushed it off her shoulders then began to make short work of her skirt.

By the time I backed into my sad little bed, I had her down to her bra and panties. I was still sporting my slacks, but I didn't care. I swept my hands along her, cupping her breasts and tugging her bra up and out of the way so I could tease her nipples into tight little peaks. I tugged my mouth from hers and she let out a gasp of protest that quickly turned into a low moan as I dragged my tongue along her jaw.

"God!" Her voice was breathy. "I'm so sorry I didn't believe you."

"I know."

I sat down on the bed and tugged her between my knees so I could kiss my way down her neck. I scraped my teeth against her collarbone and she sighed, her hands sweeping up over my shoulders and around my neck. I shifted my way down her chest to catch a breast in my mouth. I leaned forward against her as I lavished it with my tongue before I latched fully on the hardened peak and sucked. Her fingers sifted through my hair and with a gentle tug, I drug my mouth along the patch of skin to her other breast.

"I missed you," she gasped out, starting a light babble. Like it was something she needed to get out. "Everywhere I looked I would see a shadow of you." I set my teeth against her sensitive nipple and looked up at her face, watching as her brows went together and felt her shiver against me. "I would dream about you and wake up to my bed being empty. Like there was a hole in it and in my heart." Her eyes fluttered open, and she met my gaze. "And I'm the one that created it."

I reached behind her to unhook her bra then I pulled away long enough to strip it off of her.

"You can make it up to me," I assured her. "We all make mistakes."

Once it was out of the way I pushed her panties down her hips, running my hand down along her ass as I did. She pulled away from me and her eyes connected with me.

"I'm not going to be stupid and let go this time. I'm not going to turn away when things get scary."

"Hopefully, you don't have to worry about me getting arrested again," I assured her. "Never want to experience that again."

"I won't leave you to face it alone if it does happen again." She pressed her brow to mine. "I want to be there to support you through the hard times."

My heart sped up in my chest. Hearing her say that seemed to have the same effect as hearing her say she loved me. I tugged her onto my bed, a measly full-size thing that would make this cramped and hard to maneuver on. I flung her onto her back so I could prowl above her.

"Keep saying stuff like that," I growled at her. "And you won't ever be rid of me."

"Maybe I don't want to get rid of you," she retorted. Her breathing was heavy and she pushed her fingers into my beard until she could get a decent handful. She gave it a tug and I had no choice but to come to her. "Maybe I want to wake up every morning with you next to me."

She met me the rest of the way to give me a hungry kiss. It was like the last few weeks didn't even exist... all that shit went out the door. All that existed anymore was her and me. I wanted to reaffirm the taste of her but not just her mouth. I pulled away from her and followed the line of her throat down her chest, over her stomach, and down to the little line of curls between her thighs. She didn't resist me as she stayed stretched out across my bed. I shifted her thighs up onto my shoulders and parted her lower lips. She flushed a bright pink and I could see just how wet she was. Maybe her admitting all of this did something to her or maybe she wanted me as much as I wanted her. I rolled my tongue over the length of her slit, tracing it up to the little bundle of nerves at the top. She twitched and moaned; her hands went into my hair and tugged as her hips began to roll up against my mouth.

I knew she liked this and I understood why. Having her lips wrapped around my cock those weeks before was pure heaven. I worked two fingers into her and watched as she threw her head back, moaning aloud at how good it felt. My name was like a prayer flowing from her lips and I decided I wanted to hear it again. I reached up to stroke her breasts just as I sucked her clit into my mouth. Her hips bucked against my face in response and I used my teeth to make her whimper before I soothed her with light swipes of my tongue. I wasn't sure how long I stayed between her knees, but it was well past the time that she clenched around my fingers and cried out at just how much she loved me. I pulled my fingers from her and pressed my tongue into her quivering hole, savoring her flavor.

She clenched and I felt her hands tugging at my hair. "Please, it's too much."

That was enough I decided, and I pulled away from her sweet cunt. I wiped my mouth on the back of my hand and looked down at her.

"I don't have any condoms here, Sweetcheeks." It was probably for the best to admit it. "Left 'em all at your house."

She tugged me down to her, her arms going around my neck and her hips pressed against mine. It was then I realized I still had fucking slacks on. She left a damp spot from where she rocked up against my clothed dick. If I wasn't going to need to get the suit cleaned before, I would definitely need to now. But, fuck it; it's hard to resist a beautiful woman thrusting against you.

"I don't care," she breathed, reaching down the tug at my belt. "I want you. I want you in me." She kissed me, sweeping her tongue against my lips and I'm sure she got a generous tasting of her cum still clinging to my face. "Before everything happened," she had my belt open and was working on the buttons of the pants, "I got on birth control. I have an implant in my arm." My brows went up, and I pulled away to look at her. "Before I wanted to feel every bit of you and wanted nothing between us." Her voice shook a little as she looked up at me. "I still want that. I want nothing between us and I want you... if you can forgive me for abandoning you." She seemed to be searching my expression. "I want to give you everything that I have."

"I want it," I assured her, letting her press the slacks that were only slightly too big for me. "I want you, I want everything. I'm going to take it all and give you everything in return."

As soon as she got my dick free and the pants down around my ankles, she started stroking me. She made sure she had me to the point of throbbing, and I lowered myself down. As I got close, she aimed me into her sopping wet entrance. Nothing was between us as I started to ease into her, just the tight heat of her giving in. There was no barrier preventing me from feeling the silky wetness and the only lubricant was her. I groaned and buried my face against her throat.

"I'm not going to be able to use condoms again."

"I don't want you to." Her breath was shaky. "I want to feel all of you. Every bit of you in me."

I thrust forward so that my cock became fully seated in her and it was all I could do to not bust it right then.

"You keep talking like that," I started, grunting as her muscles fluttered around me. "And this is going to be embarrassingly short."

I propped myself up on my elbows and she leaned forward to kiss me again. Words became secondary as anything else said was a babbled mess of feelings that just seemed to pour out unfiltered. I found a rhythm steadily enough, taking a little time to adjust to the feel of her and the throbbing flutter of her muscles. Her thighs latched onto my hips and her legs were wrapped around me just as tightly as her cunt. It left little wiggle room, and if I had the dumb idea of needing to escape, I would have to fight for it. She held onto me like I was a life raft; like she was drowning the sensation of each raw thrust.

Condoms are definitely overrated. I couldn't even remember if I ever had the opportunity to fuck a girl raw, but here I was swearing into her ear that I would worship her forever for just the opportunity to fuck her like this. Her fingers curled into my hair and she was gasping out how good it felt again. She was wringing my cock almost painfully. It felt so good.

I managed to keep going, even as her nails dug into my back and shoulders. I worked my way through the choking hold she had on me until I felt her gush around my cock. It was the most delicious feeling and I stopped for a beat as she quaked around me, her cries going unfettered. It was enough for me to realize there was some truth to her words. She missed me just as much as I missed her; this was more than just sex or fucking. Hell, she admitted she loved me. Even as she came down from the high of the orgasm that just rolled through her, I heard reverent whispers of 'I love you' tickling my ear.

I let out a long groan and began thrusting again, my balls felt heavy and I knew it wouldn't be long. But there was something extra about riding out her orgasm that I just wanted to enjoy that heated embrace. I pressed my forehead to her shoulder and put a bit more force behind my hips. I wouldn't last long, but I was going to go out with a fucking bang. Her fingers scraped against my skin and I could feel her trembling around me as I forged ahead harder.

"Everything," I bit out next to her ear. "I want it all."

"Yes," she moaned in response.

"Me and you, through thick and thin," I growled and sat up on my knees, my hands going to her hips as I ground against them. "You don't get to bail when shit hits the fan and gets scary. You understand?"

She nodded, her face flushed and her gaze blurred. "Not going... anywhere," she said between gasps.

"I don't care if this is still new," I huffed and kept pounding into her. "I will..." The shakes started, and I tried to hold on as I could feel everything getting tight. "Be putting a ring..." I gritted my teeth, I didn't want to come just yet. "On this!" I gasped then seized as I exploded into her.

I saw stars and it was all I could do to not fall forward onto her. I melted down, trying my best to keep from putting too much weight on her. My hips jerked as it felt like I just poured three weeks worth of come into her. It had been that fucking long.

"God..." I hissed, still feeling the throbbing as my dick started to go soft. "...damn." I shifted to kiss her face. "That was too fucking long to go without this," I winced and licked the side of her mouth. "Fucking torture, woman."

"I'm sorry." She panted under me, making no move to wiggle out of my grasp. Her inner muscles loosened their hold on me, and she rolled her hips as she seemed to enjoy me just being in her. "I promise it won't--"

A bang on my bedroom wall interrupted her, and we both jerked to look up at it. "That's enough," a voice boomed on the other side. "Some people have to go to work in the morning!"

I felt her tense underneath me and I punched the wall. "Fuck off, Jerry," I hollered back. "I don't bitch when you get laid." She looked up at me wide-eyed, her brows pulled up so high they nearly touched her hairline. "Neighbor." I could only shrug. "This place is cheap, so the walls are paper thin."

She nodded and blinked slowly as she seemed to understand what I was saying. "I guess that means we'll have to just get you out of here." Her gaze went serious as she tugged me closer. "We never had anyone beating on the walls at my place," she pointed out. "Maybe that's just where we need to put you?"

"That mean you're going to give me my key back?" I asked curiously.

She started to run her fingers through my beard, using her fingers to clean the residue of her cum from it. "You get your key back," she said lightly. "And if you want to take your things to my place, all your things not just a few pieces of clothing, I wouldn't object."

I snorted slightly, trying not to laugh at the idea she was proposing. "You mean you want me to move in?"

"I think I remember you being there all the time when we first started dating anyway." She paused to kiss me lightly. "Besides it's not half as serious as you putting a ring on it."

"Let's see how this goes with me moving in," I said as she paused in kissing me. "If we can hack living together, then I'll put a ring on it. We'll discuss details later." I took her lip between my teeth and narrowed my eyes at her. "I think I feel a second wind coming on." I didn't give her a chance to protest. I rolled us over so that she was on top. "You ready to make it up to me?"

She gasped out and sat up, sitting back on my thighs and feeling my growing hardness in her. "Wh-what about your neighbor?"

"Fuck Jerry." I put my hands on her hips and thrust up into her experimentally. I wasn't fully hard, but with the way she clamped around me, I knew it wouldn't take me long to get that way. "You liked fucking me this way before." I rolled my hips against hers, and I saw her brows go together at the feeling of my pubic bone rubbing against her clit. "Or we can shift this around, and I can throw it into you from behind. You like it that way, too, if I remember correctly."

"Yes," she breathed, and as her hands went down to rest on my stomach, she started to move with me. "Maybe," her breath hitched, "we can try both ways."

"I ain't going to jail," I assured her. "We got all day to cycle through every position you like."

There was nothing like that knowledge that you had nothing keeping you from throwing it into the girl you loved.

27

It had taken some serious convincing on my part, but after I moved in with her and we managed a routine, I had finally worn her down. Not that it didn't take effort. There were still some serious talks about consequences and how safety was important. But I won out in the long run. That was something I was still celebrating as I sat on my bike, holding it up and letting it purr between my thighs. I looked at her, raising an eyebrow daring her.

"You still chicken?"

Madi stood at the edge of her porch, looking nervous. She was wearing a pair of skinny jeans that emphasized the curves of her hips and thighs in the most delicious way. She had on a tank top and my riding jacket on over that, even though it swallowed her whole. I wasn't going to be careless with her. She was far too important.

"You promise not to go too fast, right?"

"I won't go faster than the speed limit," I assured her, pulling a spare helmet from a saddlebag. "I love this bike about as much as I love you. I ain't gonna do anything stupid on it."

I hoped she understood. A man's bike was almost as important as his old lady. I watched her blush, and she came down the final steps to meet me in the driveway. She took the helmet from me and I helped her put it on. It needed some adjusting and I found that I'd probably need to get another one that fit her properly before we did any serious riding. I had visions of Sturgis with her on the back of my bike. If I could sucker her on it now, I could only imagine how much more fun a rally would be with her.

"That's going to have to do for now," I grimaced as I noticed it wasn't as snug as it should be. She'd need a riding jacket that fit her, too. "You ready to get on?"

"Ready as I'll ever be," she breathed, the nervousness in her green eyes made them so bright. She had been tempted to put contacts in but it took one mention of bugs to convince her that glasses were the way to go. "You promise you'll be safe?"

I grabbed her hand and tugged her close. "I want to keep you with me forever," I growled over the purr of my motorcycle. "I'm not going to be able to do that if I do something stupid and we have an accident. Do you get me? I need you safe and sound, so I'm going to be safe."

She nodded, and I helped her onto the bike behind me, tugging her knees into position so that she was pulled tight against me. She shifted and gasped, the vibrations seeming to affect her predictably. I couldn't keep from grinning. "Hold on to me, wrap your arms around me and if I lean a certain way, lean with me."

"O-okay." Her voice shook, and her arms came around my waist and held me tight.

"I'm going to get us going slow through the neighborhood. If you don't freak out, I'll take us out in town." I threw a smirk back at her before I started the bike forward.

She yelped sharply as her hands dug into my shirt and her thighs tightened around my hips. She didn't cry out for me to stop, she just clung to me harder with each turn we took. There was nothing better than feeling the length of her pressed against my back. I wouldn't trade this for anything. No matter the fact that we had relations beforehand, I could feel my dick getting hard again.

I kept our ride short because the roar of the engine and the sound of the road made it difficult to hear anything. If she had complaints I wanted to be able to hear them, it had taken a great deal of time to soothe her fears about taking this ride. I took us to the bar, and when I rolled us to a stop and cut the engine, she gasped in surprise.

"Why did you stop?"

I tried not to laugh as I pulled my helmet off then turned to tug hers off, too. I needed to see her face.

"We got where we were going," I informed her. "Why? You want a longer ride?"

"If I decide this is for keeps, I get to ride with you anytime I want, right?" She asked, her eyes were bright behind her smudged glasses, and I could tell the same bug that had bitten me had bitten her, too.

I felt my heart pick up in my chest and I looked at her hard. "You want me for keeps now?"

She tugged me back against her, and I felt her lips against my ear. "I liked you in the beginning and I can honestly say you grew on me with little effort." Her teeth tugged at the lobe of my ear, and I groaned as I felt my cock started to perk up to attention. "Now I want you for keeps."

"Shit." I handed her the helmet back. "I was going to take us out on a nice social outing, now you're telling me I've got to take you back home and put you to bed. I'm getting so many mixed signals," I complained in jest, after hearing all of that I couldn't wait to get ball deep into her.

"But, I didn't," she started to argue. "I didn't say to take me back home!"

"Oh no." I put my helmet back on. "You don't get to say shit like that and not have me take you home to lay you down for some sweet lovin'. Nope, you say you want me for keeps you better be prepared for me to bend you over."

I heard her laugh even as I kicked my bike back to life and turned to take us back to her place. Our place… she had made it so it wasn't just her place anymore. She made it our place.

"Now you're never going to be rid of me."

28

I pulled over onto the side of the highway, having had to piss for the last five miles and the vibrations of my silver lady just wasn't helping. I helped Madi off and hobbled to the edge of the woods before pulling out to get some much needed relief. I couldn't help but groan as I let out a steady stream.

"Your ability to urinate out in the open is disturbing," Madi commented from behind me.

"Have you heard the neighbors complaining yet?" I glanced over my shoulder, saw her expression and couldn't help but cackle at it.

While I hadn't actually done it, it was funny to see her stare at me in disbelief. She thought I'd actually done it.

"I'm lucky I haven't gotten any complaints about your motorcycle... are you really going to add you pissing out in the yard to my concerns?" she frowned at me.

I gave myself a shake before I put the boy away and zipped up. "I gotta mark my territory," I sauntered up to where she stood propped against my bike. "You know, I got this hot thing waiting for me and I got to make sure no one gets any ideas."

I needed a kiss. I couldn't resist the urge when I saw a sexy smile curling along her lips. We hadn't taken off our helmets, so we ended up knocking heads when I tried to go in for one. It made her laugh out loud and it was one of the best sounds I could have heard from her.

"You ready to get back on the road?" I asked, pulling my bike up from her kickstand.

"Are you ready to get back on the road? We've been driving for about an hour. How are you holding up?"

There was concern on her face and her need for me to be alright just seemed to give me further drive.

"I'm good," I smiled, trying to alleviate her concern. "We still got another two hours before we get where we're going. I took my drugs, I can handle another couple of hours."

She nodded. Curiosity probably kept her from arguing with me, but she looked worried. I helped her get settled on the bike and then I mounted it in front of her. I started it up and got us back on the road. I hadn't told her where we were going and I intended to keep it a surprise. I wanted to take her breath away. I wanted to knock her on her ass with the beauty I was about to show her so when it was all said and done, she wouldn't have any idea what was coming.

Madi kept her arms around me, hugging me from behind and pressing along the length of my back. She had gotten over her initial fear of riding on my bike and even got the itch to go for rides once in a while. More often than not, when I wasn't busy with the shop she would come find me and whisper in my ear, "Let's go for a ride." If I thought I loved her before, I was so far gone that there wasn't a chance for me now.

The time we spent apart after my arrest was like water under the bridge. She made a huge effort to make me feel at home in her house... our house. The last year had been a learning process between the two of us, getting adjusted to living with another person and respecting each other's space. Even though we were together, there was something about living with another person that you had to figure out. I had experience from living in the barracks that seemed to have prepared me for anything. I got the feeling that Madi didn't. I had to give her space like silence for when she wanted to curl up with a book and a cup of coffee.

Figuring out the relationship deal was harder than I was prepared for, but so far we made it work. We pushed our comfort levels and she made me realize just how damn smart she was. I had the unfortunate occurrence of bad days and she was there to scrape me up to cart me to the VA when shit just got to be too much. But as far as I was concerned, with the good times and the bad, we were together for keeps. She didn't argue that one bit either.

We road along the 220 in silence, mostly because it was kind of hard to have a good conversation while riding a motorcycle. I could feel her turn and twist when we road through Roanoke to take in the sights of the city. I should have slowed down or stopped so she could explore, but I had other plans. I had to get us somewhere special before dark and any long breaks would have messed with my plans. Some things I couldn't avoid, like when we rode up on the Natural Bridge Park one of my secrets came out. I heard an audible gasp from her and her arms tightened around my middle. I made sure to slow enough that she wouldn't miss the scenery and I parked when I had to. I was stiff from the ride up here and our hike was more of a slow hobble. She had patience with me, waiting for me when I had to try to shake out the pain so we could keep moving. But as soon as we came across the natural bridge I lost her. She drifted close to the railing and looked up at the mass of rock that was suspended above us. Her eyes were huge as she looked at the graffiti laden walls beneath it. I held her hand and let her lead me along as she explored the outcrop of rocks. I had a hunch she would enjoy something like this.

I hadn't gotten my chance to take her to Sturgis. That was too long of a bike ride for me to make, but I made sure I took her as far as I could when I could. Madi wasn't the type to hang on and close her eyes while we went on rides either. I'd see her looking around and taking in everything while she clung to me. She had a sense of adventure. It was low key, but she would marvel at everything we came across on our trips no matter where we ventured to.

I had a reason for bringing her out here though. It was crammed into my pocket and it was weighing me down as I trailed behind her. I just needed a good moment to spring it on her but I didn't want to distract her from what she was looking at. I had an idea of what she would say and I had a plan for how things would go after I dropped it on her. So, I needed her to get her fill of this place before we wandered back to the room I booked for us. The lights had kicked on to put more emphasis on the bridge above us.

"This was what you wanted to bring me to?" she stopped and looked back at me, her green eyes were huge behind her glasses and I could see the wonder shining back at me.

"Yep," I gave her a grin.

"You're up to something," her brows drew together and she looked like she was ready to grill me. "What is it?"

"I'll tell you," I ventured closer so I could get that kiss I wanted before.

I nipped at her bottom lip before I hungered for more. She opened for me and seemed to sigh as soon as I got a good taste of her. She leaned in and let me plunder her mouth until all my aches and pains were forgotten except for the throbbing one I had pressed against her.

"Question is," I murmured against her mouth. "Do you want it now or later?"

Her breath hitched and I felt her roll her hips against mine. Sex usually ensued after bike rides. It was something that seemed to get her going and I was happy to oblige her when I could. I was also happy to find out that the length of the trip didn't seem to cool her libido at all. Lucky me.

"Now," she breathed. "As fantastic as all this is," she admitted lightly, "there's pretty much only one thing I can think of doing now. I'm pretty sure you can guess what it is."

"I dunno," I grinned because there was nothing more fun than making her say it. She didn't like to talk dirty but I could get it out of her. And when I managed to draw it out of her, it came pouring out. "Maybe you should tell me."

"I want you," her voice was a low purr and the sound went straight to my dick.

"You want me?" I taunted. "What do you want from me?"

I got a huff from her but she didn't pull away. Sooner or later I'd get her to tell me without prompting.

"I want you," she took hold of the lapels of my cut and tugged me close as her whisper turning into a growl, "to fuck me. If that means I have to drag you into the woods to get you to fuck me I will."

If I hadn't already been sporting a hard-on, that right there would have gotten all the blood rushing to my cock, still I was a little dizzy.

"Well, shit," I said. "I guess I need to do this first then."

I started to fall down on one knee.

"What are you doing?" then she began to panic. "Are you okay? Are you hurting? I knew the ride was going to long, Sid!"

I let her fuss over me as I got on my good knee and tugged a little velvet box from my pocket.

"Hey," I said sharply when I saw her green eyes start to look watery. "I'm fine," I gave her a hard look. "Stop worrying about me and listen," her brows drew together and she focused her attention on my face rather than the position I was in. "We started out rough, shit got serious and shaky quick," I cleared my throat when I felt it start to tighten. "But we put that behind us and managed to move forward without as many bumps in the road," I brought the box to her attention and I watched as her eyes got as big as saucers. "I want to keep going forward with you. I kept telling you I was going to put a ring on it," I opened the box so she could see the ring. It wasn't impressive, not something that would weigh her hand down. It was a simple round solitaire, but when I saw it I knew immediately it was the one so I scrimped and saved for it. "Marry me?"

She made a choking noise and for a split gut wrenching second I thought she was going to turn me down. I felt the tears burning behind my eyes and it took everything for me to stay in that kneeling position.

"Are you kidding? Of course!" she tugged me forward and I was pressed between her breasts.

Now I was choking up, it's funny how uncertainty can do that to you. Thank God, was all I could think. Thank fucking God. She covered my face in kisses, pressing her lips on my brow and then my cheeks. I tilted my face up so I could catch her mouth as it traveled along my face.

"Help me up," I grunted. "Then I can put this ring on you so we can go to the hotel and fuck as much as you want."

She quickly pulled me to my feet and then launched herself into my arms as soon as I was stable. She kissed me hungrily and I couldn't help but tug away from her. I removed the ring from the box and chucked the velvet container. I took up her left hand and slid the ring onto her finger. It seemed like something was falling into place, everything seemed to be coming together with my life. She seemed to be mesmerized by the ring on her finger, her green eyes large and watery again.

"You're not going to cry, are you?"

"I'm happy," she assured me and I relaxed. "I didn't think I would get this, ever," her breath hitched as she spoke. "I thought I blew my chance with a great guy last year and here you are."

"I told you I was going to put a ring on it," I said, thinking maybe she doubted me. "I didn't change my mind."

"Thank you," she kissed me sweetly and I almost felt just how much she loved me in that one kiss.

I pressed my brow to hers, "Let's get to the hotel so I can take care of my old lady."

"Is that what you're going to call me?" she started tugging me back in the direction of where I had parked my bike.

"That's what you are, Sweetcheeks."

I was light as air and could barely feel the walk back. After all the stress, planning, and saving, this came together so easily. No hiccups. I had been so afraid she'd say no.

We made it back to my bike and she tugged me to a halt before I could even get back onto it. My gut went cold, thinking she was having second thoughts. But when I looked at her, I saw her give the area a cautious glance. It had grown dark and while there were lights on the natural bridge it was pretty evident that we were the only ones out here. Madi met my gaze and I knew we were about to have the fun kind of trouble. She stepped against me, threading fingers through my beard.

"How quiet can you be?"

"Baby, we're in a canyon. I'm gonna yell my throat raw just so I can hear the echoes if you're wanting to get nasty here," I growled low at her. "You want me to fuck you out in the open like this? I'll do it, but there's a real good chance we'll get caught."

I saw a moment of indecision... she wanted me and she wanted the thrill of sex out in the open. Since we'd been knocking boots on a regular basis she had started getting more and more adventurous with where and how she liked it. I thought back to what I had said to Jimmy when I first laid eyes on her, "never judge a book by its cover." Her free hand started working my belt loose and it thrilled me how much she wanted this.

"Don't yell too much," she warned me with a hard look before she dropped down to her knees.

I didn't give her a reason to change her mind or get mad, hell, I didn't make a sound until she had my cock out and in her hand. I kept a lookout as she started to draw me into the sweet heat of her mouth. All bets were off then, I groaned as she started swallowing me, her tongue working the underside of my cock in a steady rhythm. I tilted my head back and rocked my hips towards her sweet mouth, letting her build me up until I was throbbing.

"I'm gonna cum," I choked out, thinking if she was serious about sex out here she needed to stop before I went busting down her throat.

She either ignored me or didn't hear me, betting on the ignored part. One of her hands cupped my balls and began to roll them gently while the other worked my length as she shifted to just suck on the head of my cock. I peered down to meet her sexy gaze and I knew that's where she wanted it.

"Fuck," I gritted out before all the stimulation became too much for me to take. My hips jerked forward, shoving more of my cock into her mouth just as I exploded into it. I let out a long groan that echoed around us, "Sweet fucking Jesus! That's good." I was a chatty fucker when it came to shit like this.

Madi was sweet enough to swallow and clean me up before she tucked me back into my jeans.

"You have got until we get to the hotel to get hard again," she commanded as she stood. She tugged our helmets out of the saddlebags and put one in my hands. "I hope you're ready to spend the next couple of days celebrating the fact that you finally put a ring on it."

"Girl," I snorted as I put my helmet on, still riding that wave of euphoria, "I'm gonna make it so you walk funnier than I do."

We mounted my bike and I found myself rushing to the historic hotel that sat just outside the national park. I thought for a second that I lost her when we walked in, her eyes were huge again. I let her wander as I checked us in. Madi liked things like this; old things, anything historic really. I watched her marvel at a display case before she looked up at me. I knew then that I'd have to plan another adventure like this. I'd have to take her to some out of the way stop so I could see that expression she was shining at me now.

"You ready to go upstairs or do you wanna look some more?"

"How long are we going to be here?"

"Check out is Sunday by eleven," I said lightly, because it wasn't really a big deal to me. "That'll give us plenty of time to explore the park and the hotel."

She came closer to me, just within reach without actually touching me.

"Let's go upstairs then," her voice was calm, but her cheeks were flushed.

I had a feeling that it wouldn't be long before she would come find me so we could pick up where we left off. Fortunately, we were on the bottom floor, I didn't want to be stuck struggling up stairs every time we decided to go somewhere. If we went anywhere, it seemed as soon as I got the door opened and us in the room, she had every intention of keeping me busy.

She kissed me hungrily, her hands going into my hair and tugging me close. Her tongue circled around mine and I savored the taste of her mouth, I shifted so I had her against the wall. She arched my hips against hers, not quite having made a rebound from the love she gave me earlier. One of her legs hooked around my hip and I ground against her, trying to see if ole' boy was ready for the real thing. I got half-mast when I decided I would just give her something to squeal about for a bit. I pulled away from her grasp with some effort and walked to the king sized bed that took up the majority of the room. I shrugged off my cut then tugged my shirt over my head, feeling her eyes drift over me as I undressed.

"Do me a favor, Sweetcheeks. Get naked and c'mere," I pulled off my belted and unbuttoned my jeans before I sat down.

"You're lucky you're cute," she said to me as she started to kick off her shoes.

"Yea?"

I tore off my boots and leaned back on the bed, watching as she tugged up her t-shirt to expose the lovely lacy bra she wore. I hummed as she exposed more of herself to me, pushing the jeans off her hips and giving me an amazing view of her creamy thighs. The more I saw of her the harder I got.

"Yea," she grunted back.

She kept her panties and bra on, they were white and gave the false impression that she was pure. I knew better since I enjoyed every chance I got to be between her thighs.

"Otherwise, I wouldn't let you call me that," she prowled onto the bed with me, moving so that she was hovering over me. "Nothing like hearing about my sweet ass all the time," she trailed off as a hand moved up my stomach, her fingers tracing line and perking up the interest of my pecker.

"Well it is a sweet ass," I didn't hesitate to reach around to get myself a handful. I used it as a way to pull her against me, on top of me, wanting to feel every curve on me. "I love this sweet ass," I grinned as I caught her mouth, kissing her hungrily.

I decided to keep that hand on her ass and tangled the other in her hair as I put her into the position that I wanted her. Her hips were rolling against mine even with her focus seeming to be completely on mouths. I shifted my hand into her panties, raking my fingernails against her skin as I considered how I wanted her.

"How do you want this?" I decided I wanted her to say it, I arched my hips up into hers so there was no confusing my meaning.

She liked being on top and I had my own preferences, depending on how I was feeling. She also enjoyed it from behind. That's how I got the most noise from her. She sat up and rolled her hips against mine, feeling how hard my erection had gotten as she considered which way she wanted to take it. Her thrusts against me kept going and I could see she was getting into the prospect of the position she was in.

"Keep this up and I'm gonna cum in my pants," I complained.

"Can't have that," she shifted back onto my thighs and tugged my jeans down.

"What, no foreplay?"

"The ride over here was foreplay," she murmured, wiggling deliciously against me as she got out of her panties. "The vibrations of the bike and being pressed against you," she purred as she positioned me at her entrance. I could instantly feel the slick heat.

She wasn't lying to me, though if I thought real hard about it, I would probably remember all the times that going for a ride led to something sexy. I couldn't argue with her logic though, it gave me the same feels. I couldn't get sick of the feeling of her sinking down on my cock, taking every inch of me into that tight hold.

Once I was fully seethed, I reached up to push her bra out of the way, wanting to see her tits bounce with each thrust she made. I watched as she tilted backward, shifting the angle that I went into her at. I watched her bite her lip as she struggled to hold in a groan. I couldn't have it, I wanted it hear all of it. I bucked my hips up into hers and she gasped out, I reached up to cup her chin.

"Don't be quiet," I growled at her. "Let all of it out."

She whined, looking as if she wanted to deny me, but I wasn't going to give her the opportunity. My hands went to her hips and with a little effort began to thrust up into her. She threw her head back and moaned as I ground into that sweet spot with each thrust that I made. The second wind I had gotten since she sucked me off wasn't going to afford me much time; I could already feel the pressure building in me. She didn't give me the chance to play with her beforehand so I had to make a conscious effort to shift my fingertips down to where we were joined to play with the swollen button there. She caught me up in a strangling hold then, rocking forward as she got all the more closer to her sweet end. Her fingers ticked at my stomach, seeming to look for something to hold onto as I rammed myself up into her. I gave her clit a sharp pinch, because I didn't know how much longer I could take her squeezing me without exploding. I heard a sharp gasp that sounded like my name, her muscles pulsed in time with my heart beat and the dampness started to dribble out making it slicker. Each thrust became easier to throw up into her. I wanted her close now, I wanted to feel her breasts against my chest. I wanted to kiss her. I sat up and wrapped my arms around her, pressing my brow to hers.

"I love you," I said. No matter what I did, it came out every time we were intimate like this.

She held onto me, riding out her orgasm as I kept on thrusting my hips up into hers. Her gaze was blurry and her brows were drawn together.

"I love you," was echoed back to me.

"This is me and you," I grunted as I struggled to keep from letting it all go. "I got your back, you got my back, right?"

She nodded, her blurry eyes going glassy in minutes. "Yes," it came out with conviction. "Not going anywhere, I'm here to ride out all the rough patches with you."

Her breath hitched and her nails dug into my back, I could feel her getting closer to another orgasm with the hold on my cock tightening again.

"I love you," her voice hardened, as if she thought I doubted her.

"Good," I flipped us, putting her onto her back so I could get at a better position to thrust into her. "Because I ain't going anywhere, now," I grunted. "I put a ring on it, I'm gonna cart your ass down the aisle and make you Mrs. Redding. You got me?"

"Yes!"

Her voice was as sharp as her nails in my back and I started to tremble, I couldn't hold it off anymore. I bared my teeth and ground into her hard. It was too much, all of it was too much. The emotions gripping my heart making my chest hard, the pulsing heat of her cunt strangling my cock, and the sweet chant she started to take up. She loved me. This was it for the both of us and there was no turning back. I let out a low groan as I erupted inside her, managing a last jerky thrust before I melted against her.

Things got a little fuzzy and I might have dropped off into a doze. She had me surrounded, her hands drifting through my hair and her legs curled around my hips loosely. This was relaxing and as close to home as a man could get.

"I'm a man of my word," I mumbled against her neck.

"You do nothing but prove it," she sighed and kissed my temple. "Now that you put a ring on it, what do you intend to do now?"

"Get old and gray and fuck you as much as I can," I grinned and drug my teeth along her skin. I rubbed my beard against her chest and neck until she started to squeal and wiggle under me. "Got any complaints to that?"

"No," she gasped out. "Please," her arms flailed from around me. "I give! You got me!"

"Good," I smirked down at her. "I'm not letting go either." I caught her mouth in a kiss and shifted us so that we were laying on our sides. This felt like a big step into the right direction, I could only imagine how good the bigger picture looked.

SCARLET LANTERN
Publishing

Other Titles by Amber Burns

The Boneyard Brotherhood

Overhaul
Enforcer
Rebel

Biker Reverse Harem Romances

Biker Night

Standalone Bad Boy Romances

Inked Passions
Relentless Desire
The Crown Prince
The Heart of a Hero

Find all of my new releases at
www.scarletlanternpublishing.com/amberburns

Printed in Great Britain
by Amazon

77044389R00106